TESSERA
THE 47 SHADOWS

TESSERA
THE 47 SHADOWS

STEPHEN B. GRESKO

CONTENTS

PROLOGUE

A JOURNEY OF A THOUSAND miles must begin with taking a single, small, courageous step in not just the right direction but in any direction at all. These words resounded in the mind of the sleeping child. He always knew he was destined for great things, or rather that was always what he had been told. But within the dreams of this young boy, he felt as if that was wrong. He was not destined for greatness at all.

Walking down the endless corridor of his own mind, the boy looked all around at what filled the unfamiliar walls. These walls formed and supported his own being—he was them and they were him, yet they still felt so foreign to him.

Covering them were pictures of people he knew, places he had been, memories of events long since passed. However, mixed in with the familiar were things the boy could not seem to place. The distorted smile on the face of a beloved friend, an emblem on a strange uniform covered in blood, and an intense feeling of pain that he had never felt before.

All these things puzzled the boy, for he knew that this was his own mind and his alone. How could there be things here that he never remembered experiencing?

1

Confused, the boy continued to walk deeper, determined to find what lay at the end of the hallway. Whether it be a person, a moment, or an object, he did not know. The boy had always thought the direction of his life was set, but all these strange visions sparked a new train of thought. Maybe the path wasn't as fixed as he had once believed.

Now, for the first time in his life, the boy freely chose to walk down the path as it was set before him until it reached its inevitable conclusion and, hopefully, the answers to his questions. Turning back now was never even a thought in his mind.

After what seemed like an eternity, or perhaps only just a moment, he could hear a distant ringing sound. At that same moment, he saw a faint light emanating from two silhouettes that suddenly materialized, blocking the pathway before him.

The boy could not make out their faces, but he could see their outstretched hands reaching towards him. Believing this was what he had been searching for, he rushed forward, hand outstretched, without a single reservation. The only thing repeating in his mind was *I can reach them. I must reach them.*

Just as he was about to take hold of the two figures' hands, there came a deafening sound, and he closed his eyes to a blinding light. Before he could open his eyes once more, it was all over.

1

FROM THE DEPTHS
OF A DREAM

O PENING HIS WEARY EYES, Leo's surroundings slowly came back into focus. Lazily looking around his environment, it appeared to be slightly different than what he remembered from the night before.

His room was flipped from the normal perspective he was used to. Slowly coming to, he also realized that the ceiling seemed to be much farther away than he remembered it being. He also noticed that he felt very different from normal. His back was very cold, unlike the usual feeling when in his nice warm bed. As the morning fog began to clear from Leo's mind, he sat up, finally realizing why everything seemed off. Was he on the floor?

Scratching his head, he looked up at his bed. He must have rolled off during the night and been in such a deep sleep that he didn't even notice. While Leo was putting the pieces of his strange night together, he heard the mechanical sound of his bedroom door open with a hiss as a young boy in a uniform casually strolled inside like he owned the place.

"Yo, you're not awake yet??" the boy said, his voice full of surprise.

Leo wiped the sleep from his eyes. "Yeah, I am now; thanks, Locke."

Locke couldn't help looking down on Leo with a half-disappointed and half-amused expression. "You're supposed to be our leader and all, yet here you are. Laying so casually on the floor and in such a sad state. You're lucky it's just me who found you like this and not the others."

Trying to hide his smug grin, Locke walked over and hit the alarm next to Leo. He had been in such a daze that Leo hadn't realized that it had been going off the entire time on the desk beside the empty bed.

For as long as he could remember, almost every morning had started the same way for Leo. He was the responsible one, who got his friends up and ready for the day, their group's leader, the role model of all his peers. It was his responsibility to always set a proper example for those around him. But ever since the "alarm clock incident," when his friend had broken his old, prized alarm clock, managing to send everyone involved to the hospital, Leo had been having trouble waking up on time. Hence the uninvited guest now standing smugly over Leo in his disheveled state.

He got up, embarrassed, and contemplated what the faces of his other friends would look like and what they would have thought if they found him in such an unceremonious position. Especially his friend Luke, who was always very strict when it came to rules and etiquette.

"You'd better hurry and get yourself presentable," Locke said. "Of all the days for you to sleep in and be late, today has to be one of the worst."

Locke's words made Leo remember what today was, for it was

a very special day, a rare day of celebration. Today was the anniversary of the founding of their home.

It was one of the few holidays that were celebrated by the adults and children who lived with Leo and Locke within the facility. It was an important day indeed, which made Leo even more embarrassed by his own forgetfulness. Even more so because he was going to be an important member of the celebration this time.

He somehow managed to get himself ready faster than he ever thought possible. He consolidated many of the more tedious steps into one, such as showering, teeth brushing, and using the toilet. As long as everything got done, why should the "how" matter?

Before Locke could even finish straightening up Leo's belongings scattered all over the floor, Leo was in his uniform, ready to go.

Finally ready to leave, Leo and Locke looked over each other's appearance to make sure everything was in order. Leo removed a piece of lint visible against the navy blue of Locke's uniform. For either of them to be even slightly disheveled was unacceptable. If that would ever be the case, they would surely be reprimanded by their teachers and, quite possibly, even the colonel. As far as being punished went, Leo and the others were always careful to avoid the harsh, piercing gaze of the colonel at any cost.

Content with their appearances, Leo swiped his ID card at the terminal, and the door slid open again with a mechanical hiss.

Unheard from inside Leo's bedroom, right outside the door was a lively throng of people, in a variety of Tessera Corporation uniforms, going about their daily business in the spacious hallway. Many were pushing carts filled with mysterious technological equipment or other more mundane supplies.

Each taking a deep breath, they moved into the hall and seamlessly mingled with the crowd and began their long walk towards the facility's Grand Academy.

"So what class is first this morning?" Locke said. "I know our schedule is different due to the celebration later."

Leo rolled his eyes. "You never listen, do you? Ms. Meli said it yesterday. The only class today is History." Conversations between the two normally ended in this fashion, Leo concerned as Locke just looked aimlessly into the distance.

As they approached the end of the hallway, the doors to one of the lifts opened. Almost in anticipation of their arrival, a rather imposing man in a suit stepped out and greeted them. Though his voice sounded cheerful, his eyes were sharp as he looked down on them.

"*Well, well, well* . . . What good timing! I was just looking for you two."

Unlike most of the people Leo and Locke dealt with daily, the director of the facility was not wearing the signature uniform of Tessera, nor a lab coat like those walking nearby. Instead, he wore a pristine suit and tie, and a very expensive-looking one at that. The only indication he belonged in the facility at all was the Tessera insignia emblazoned on his jacket pocket, as well as the rank displayed on his left shoulder. Leo thought it odd for his rank to be on nonmilitary-issue clothing.

Standing there, William A. Anderson gave off an unmistakable air of authority and power. Not necessarily physical power, but the power to sway the hearts and minds of anyone he set his eyes on, the unspoken ability of the director for the entirety of Tessera's easternmost facility.

The director smiled. "I wanted to be the first person to wish you two a happy Founding Celebration, for without you amazing children this whole facility wouldn't be possible."

Leo and Locke exchanged a quick glance and then spoke in practiced unison. "Thank you, sir!"

Leo was quite taken aback by the director's statement, for the man was not one to give out expressions of appreciation unless he truly meant it.

"Seems you are missing one from your ranks," the director said. "I wonder where she might be? I was hoping to catch you all at the same time to give my congratulations."

Realizing what he meant, Leo and Locke turned to each other. With all the commotion this morning due to Leo being late, they had both forgotten that their third member had not met up with them as usual before heading to class.

Always quick to act when it came to dealing with people and sticky situations such as this, Locke didn't even bat an eye as he spoke up. "Oh, she went ahead of us to class. She needed to go get some supplies out of storage for the celebration later today."

Coming up with a lie on the spot came easy for Locke. He was naturally talented at the art of deception, even for his young age. He wasn't one to lie for no reason, however, and this time he had a very good one because Leo had a sneaking suspicion of where their third companion was. If his suspicion turned out to be correct, it was rather important they curtail the director's curiosity now.

Leo jumped in to further back his story. "Yeah, she had to go to school early this morning, but we will definitely let her know you praised her when we see her."

Seeming content with the answer he received, the director nodded his head and thanked the two of them. "You two are going to the academy floor, correct? I'm headed in that direction, why don't you join me in the elevator?"

Locke answered in such a natural and smooth way, not even Leo could tell it was a lie at first.

"Um . . . I'm really sorry, sir, but I just remembered we forgot something important that we were supposed to bring for the celebration later. If you wouldn't mind excusing us . . ."

In response to Locke, the director's smile never faltered as he leaned in closer to the duo. Though his face and voice remained pleasant, his demeanor became suddenly intimidating, as he loomed over the two.

"Oh . . . I understand . . . Today is such a chaotic day after all. It sure is easy to forget things. Just be sure you two aren't late for the start of your studies, or there will be swift punishment, even for the likes of you two."

The director looked down at them with an ominous smirk as he finally turned and walked back into the elevator. Just as the doors were beginning to close, he stopped them and said, "After all, many of us here are watching your growth with much interest, including your long-awaited debut tonight. So, remember, eyes will always be watching your progress from the shadows. Oh, and if you do well today, I might even have a gift for the three of you. I think you'll like it very much."

Waiting until the elevator doors were completely shut, Leo and Locke turned to look at each other in a panic.

"How much time do we have before class starts???" Leo said.

"Around fifteen minutes."

"We might just be able to find her and make it there by then, but only if we run."

They both sighed as they turned their backs to the elevator and began jogging down the crowded hallway.

Expertly bobbing and weaving through the densely packed crowd of people, they still managed to carry on a conversation, a testament to how often they had to do this and just how in sync the two of them were when it came to these kinds of situations.

"Good call back there with the director!" Leo yelled, as they carefully sidestepped a tall pallet of machine parts.

"I had a feeling that since she didn't bother showing up to meet us, she probably went to that place again," Locke said, sounding half-irritated as he ducked under a large metal beam carried by two frowning men in lab coats.

"Whoa there," Leo said. "I would have to agree with you on this one. I bet she went there to goof off again. Geez, but today of all days . . . She really can be wrapped up in her own world sometimes."

Soon they came to the largest junction of the entire floor. It connected the four major hallways that made up this level. With small restaurants and stores lining the walls, it acted as a sort of communal area for people who lived and worked on this floor.

Leo and Locke always enjoyed this particular area. Leo had been told it resembled a shopping mall from the old world. Sadly, they didn't have the time to stop and smell the roses.

As soon as they made it to the center of the huge open area, they veered to the right and down another corridor. Now they were running in the direction of the floor's command center.

As the duo ran past a group of soldiers coming from the direction of the armory, one of them yelled out, "*Slow it down!* That's an order! You're going to cause an accident!"

Although Leo and Locke were of relatively high standing

within the facility, they were still lower in rank than any of the soldiers. So, begrudgingly, they slowed their run to a brisk walk as they turned yet another corner.

"Just because they wear all that gear and carry all those weapons, why do they have so much power?" Locke said.

"Well . . . Here everything is controlled by the military arm of Tessera out of sheer necessity. The outside world is an extremely dangerous place, and the military is critical to safety, not just in this facility but in all Tessera's numerous bases and installations.'"

Making eye contact, Leo and Locke laughed at Leo's recitation of the corporation's doctrine. Both of them knew very well the hierarchy of Tessera, having lived in the facility under Tessera their whole lives.

After some time, they finally reached the maintenance closet, right down the hall from the entrance to the command center. Inside, the cramped space was full of cleaning supplies and miscellaneous equipment.

After making sure the door closed behind them, Locke turned to Leo. "Now . . . where was the entrance again?"

They looked up and Leo pointed to a relatively small grate in the left corner of the ceiling. It was slightly misaligned inside its housing. However, the irregularity was so minor that no one would have noticed it in such a dark space. To Leo, however, it was a clear indication that someone had recently removed it and then haphazardly replaced it.

"Looks like she's in there after all," he said, "even though we haven't used this spot in quite some time." He looked around. "She used the rope, too."

In order to open the grate in the ceiling, they used a makeshift hook and rope to open the grate and then climb up. But with it already gone, Leo had to come up with something fast in order to get inside the ventilation shaft behind the grate. Checking his watch, he took a deep breath. They really were pressed for time.

"Locke, give me your belt while I get this clothes hook off the door. Use that tool bag if you have too."

Not even bothering to ask any questions, Locke did as he was told and took off his belt and handed it over to Leo.

"I'm going to connect our two belts together then put this hook through one of the buckles. Hopefully, they are strong enough to hold our weight." In the blink of an eye, Leo assembled the contraption and used a broom handle to move the grate aside. He tossed the homemade rope up into the hole and gave it a firm pull.

"Looks like it will hold, for now. Let's make this quick."

Leo was the first to climb up into the small hole, and then Locke quickly followed. Pulling the grate closed behind them, they moved forward through the ventilation system. They had grown since the last time they were in these vents; it was much harder to move than Leo had remembered.

"I always hated it in here," Locke said. "It's so dusty and cramped. I never understood why you guys liked to explore the ventilation system so much back in the day."

For Leo, who had an unquenchable thirst for knowledge, this was just one of the many things he used to like to explore. "It's important to firmly grasp your surroundings, even the ones you cannot directly see," he said.

The two continued their banter as they crawled down the duct. After a short distance, they reached a portion of the ventilation shaft where the bottom section was missing. This broken part of the ventilation shaft was the entrance to the trio's old "secret base."

One day while exploring this vent, a part of it collapsed underneath Leo, and he fell into a fairly decent-sized space. All around him were boxes piled high towards the ceiling. The boxes were full to the brim of everything from outdated machine parts and rusty tools to mismatched clothing. A few old documents were scattered around for good measure.

It seemed that this place was one of the many substorage spaces within the facility. However, it was apparent that it had been sealed and forgotten about long ago. Leo instantly claimed the forgotten room as his own secret hideout and showed it to his two closest friends. The fact that it was an area he was most likely not permitted in due to it being sealed off and abandoned had made it even more alluring.

They dropped out of the vent and walked deeper into the room, which was strewn with many of their old creations and childish toys. Leo spotted the homemade pair of robotic legs with an old, broken rifle mounted on top; a crude grappling hook cannon; some tiny automated vehicles; some poorly made outfits; and something the three prized above all else.

Before Leo could react, he was bum-rushed by Rusty. Displaying his unique form of doglike joy, he relentlessly assaulted Leo's face as his metallic tail wagged vigorously.

Some time ago, Lily had made the small robotic dog with old, rusted parts. On top of his lack of paint, the robotic canine just so happened to be missing his left eye. However, none of those shortcomings seemed to hinder him in the least. If anything, it only added to his excitable nature.

When Lily had initially named her creation, Leo and Locke

couldn't help but tease her. Normally she had such a convoluted naming system for her creations, but this time it just seemed to fit a little too well.

However, Leo, Lily, and Locke had never even seen a real dog before, so Rusty's programming was Lily's best rendition from all the stories they had read in their old books. But unlike the variety of canines that Rusty was based on, he was unable to bark. It was a safety measure so that no one would accidentally discover their secret companion.

"It's good to see you too, boy! Now get off!! You're getting oil all over my face."

Locke smiled and said, "You always get all the attention. I wouldn't mind getting that kind of greeting every once in a while too."

As Leo and Locke played with Rusty, Lily came out from behind one of the many towers of boxes. Waving both of her arms exuberantly, Lily called out to them. "Guuuys!! I'm almost done with the plans for my greatest masterpiece!"

"Geez, Lily, you scared us. Don't sneak up on us like that!" Locke said.

Normally she was the quietest one of the three, and she rarely ever showed this much enthusiasm. "It's fine," Leo said. "Go easy on her. You know she only gets like this if she's made a breakthrough on one of her projects."

Looking down at the mechanical dog beside him, Leo knew firsthand what Lily was capable of with just the random assorted junk in this storeroom, forget the parts used in the main facility. She was the most scientific and mechanically gifted of the three by far. At her age, her ability to turn scrap into amazing pieces of machinery was legendary within the facility.

"Lily," Leo said, "did you forget what day it is? Of all the days to come here and goof off." He walked up to her. "You realize we had to rush all the way here to get you! You understand what would happen if we were late to class, today of all days!"

"I . . . I didn't realize . . . I was so absorbed in my masterpiece; I haven't left this room all weekend." She looked at her feet.

Leo knew he had to be strict with her, for she was the most forgetful of the three. But seeing her smile and demeanor change so quickly made him feel for her.

"*Uh, it's ok . . . really . . .* Don't get like that now; we know it was just a mistake. Just try and remember these things next time so it doesn't happen again, ok?"

Lily slowly raised her head and gave a small, sad nod.

Locke gave a weary sigh. "You are always too soft on her. One of these days she's gonna mess up, and you won't be able to save her, you know."

"Well, that's why you're here, isn't it?" Leo said. "We all have each other's back. When one can't manage alone the rest of us are here to pick up the slack, aren't we?"

"Yeah . . . I guess you're right about that. As usual, you always seem to have the perfect answer."

They looked at each other, and they all grinned.

BEEP BEEP BEEP

The high-pitched sound came from Leo's wrist. Looking down at his watch, a shiver went down Leo's spine. They all knew far too well what would be waiting for them if they were tardy. "Guys, if we don't start sprinting right now, we're going to be late for Ms. Meli's class."

As they dashed for the ventilation duct, a figurative cloud of smoke was left hanging where the three used to be, as Rusty gave a lonely mechanical whimper in the now empty room.

2

HISTORY FROM
THE DISTANT PAST

AFTER RUSHING BACK THROUGH the vents, replacing the cover, and exiting the utility closet, they sprinted down the many hallways of the facility.

As the trio approached the doorway that opened to the academy wing, they slowed their pace. Leo was all too aware of the lack of other students in the area. Looking down at his watch, he breathed a long sigh. The time on it read two minutes past the hour, meaning that they would be considered tardy.

Making eye contact, they all nodded in understanding of what was to come. In all the years of them living in this facility and going to the school here, Leo could only remember ever being late to his classes just one other time.

For Leo, just that one experience was one too many. He couldn't help but shudder at the memory of the punishment he received all those years ago at the hands of Colonel Veers.

Being the commander of the facility's security forces, the colonel fittingly acted as the dean of discipline for the academy. The secretive giant of a man was seldom seen during the ordinary day-to-day of the facility.

Leo hoped not to see him now. If he were to be seen, one could be sure that someone had made a grave mistake. His nickname throughout the facility was "the Director's Fist," for he was the right hand of the director. It was well known he had eyes and ears everywhere and could deliver swift judgment to all that had the misfortune of opposing him.

Although he was a terrifying and stern individual, every resident of the facility respected him and slept easy knowing he was around. A man who could effectively protect his own people yet put the fear of god into any enemy, especially in a dangerous world such as this, was incredibly important. So, in a way, even Leo looked up to the man as a type of role model, not necessarily one he wanted to fully emulate, but one he could actively learn from.

Leo opened the door to the classroom and braced himself for the berating that was sure to come. As the trio took their first steps inside, they could see the room was filled with their peers all sitting at their desks prepared for the day's lesson, but as they quickly scanned the room their teacher was not anywhere to be found.

"Did we make it before the teacher?" whispered Lily.

"Seems like it," Locke said.

As Leo walked to his seat, he sensed something was amiss. He glanced at each student as he passed them. He couldn't figure out what was the matter, but every child seemed to be holding back a mischievous smile as he walked past.

Finally reaching his own seat, he turned to look at his friend and desk neighbor. "So, Luke, you gonna tell me what's going on?" he said, unamused.

Normally, Luke was a pretty serious person who rarely made

any kind of jokes or tried to be funny, but even he was trying his best to hold back a smile that blatantly screamed *You'd sure like to know, wouldn't you???*

Leo continued to press him for an answer, but it seemed to have the opposite effect on Luke. The more Leo tried to get the information he wanted, the more Luke tried to stifle his smile and an uncharacteristic giggle.

Having watched long enough, Locke walked over to the two and bent down to whisper something in Luke's ear.

"What are you doing???" Leo said, in an annoyed tone.

He couldn't hear what was being whispered but continued anyway. "If he won't tell me, he's not going to spill it to you either."

But spitting right in the face of Leo's previous statement, Luke began to spill the beans almost immediately after Locke pulled his head away from Luke's ear. "It . . . It's just that . . . before you came in, the director showed up, and told Ms. Meli that the three of you were going to be late to class. She then got so frustrated with you three that she stormed out almost immediately to go find out where you guys were, saying something about how dare you guys be late to her class and how you never take her class seriously."

By the end of his explanation, Luke was borderline in tears from smiling so big. "You three are in for it now! Ms. Meli is on a warpath." However, this declaration didn't surprise Leo, Lily, and Locke. They were all too familiar with the warpaths of the infamous young teacher known as Ms. Meli.

Leo and Locke had been on the receiving end of her famous tirades more than once, mostly because they rarely were interested in the class she taught, World History, since they knew almost all the information already.

Leo especially would "respectfully" debate her on many topics, which had caused many disturbances in class. Locke, on the other hand, would normally just doze off on his desk without a care in the world.

The only seemingly decent one of the three in this situation was Lily, who would be secretly building her gadgets hidden within her desk while at the same time looking as though she was completely absorbed in Ms. Meli's long lectures. Lily was indeed truly talented.

Leo wondered why the director would bother to personally come to tell Ms. Meli that they were going to be late. Did he have some idea of what they were really doing or even where they went?

As Leo was pondering this question, another occurred to him.

"*HEYY!?!? how the heck did you get that info out of Luke so easily?!?*"

Before Locke could respond, Luke interjected in a rather amused tone.

"*Well* . . . he offered to give me his piece of cake later."

Leo looked at Luke with a shocked expression, then back to Locke. "Geez, you really know how to get what you want out of people, huh?"

Locke just smiled and nodded in response.

At that moment, the door to the classroom hissed open and a disheveled individual literally skidded into the room. With only a glance, it was obvious she was in quite a fuss. Her breathing was ragged, and her hair went every which way. Simply put, this mess of a person was this classroom's teacher and actually one of the academy's head instructors, Ms. Melissa M. Meli.

She wore the standard female uniform of the facility, albeit with her own, probably against regulations, additions to it. Her messy, obnoxiously crimson hair swishing to and fro, she intently scanned the room, like a wolf hunting for its prey.

Finally spotting what she was looking for, her eyes narrowed as she placed her hands firmly on her hips. *"You three have surely done it this time!!"*

Her shrill voice resounded off all the walls in the room, creating a very unpleasant echo. The trio reflexively slouched lower in their seats, as if bracing themselves for an imminent collision.

"Even the director came to talk with me!!! That's only the third time he's ever even spoken to me, and for it to be about my students!!! The nerve of you three!"

As she continued to berate them, the other students in the room continued to hide their expressions of pleasure, for it sure was one hell of a show. Even for one as well known for her colorful tirades as Ms. Meli, this rant was an animated one, as she continued to pace while flapping her arms in a way most unbecoming of one of the academy's head instructors.

Realizing the gazes of her pupils, she planted her heels in the ground and abruptly turned to face directly at Leo. "So . . . What's your excuse for causing me all this trouble, hmmm?"

Leo had been prepared for this line of questioning, but unlike Locke, he wasn't quite a master of deception. So, eyes looking down at his desk, and in his own fashion, he told the genuine truth or at least a portion of it.

"I . . . I accidentally overslept this morning and those two had to come to wake me up. I'm truly sorry that we caused you so much trouble Ms. Meli. If you are going to punish us, please just let it be me."

Although he was an awful liar, Leo had a gift of being able to touch the hearts of others, and all she could do was stare at him with her mouth half open, as if about to say something.

In reality, he had caught her slightly off guard. She had honestly expected a much more elaborate fabrication, and shockingly, his genuine delivery made her feel almost sympathetic towards him.

Not skipping a beat though, she turned towards her desk. "I thank you for being honest with me, and for that, I will reward you. Only you shall receive punishment for being late to class, among a plethora of other things.

Suddenly remembering having to run through the halls looking for them in such a tragic state, Ms. Meli wearily smiled to herself as she turned facing away from the students.

Leo, on the other hand, semi-regretted saying such a self-righteous thing out loud. He wasn't such a just and noble person as his words would let on, but he had wagered that saying such a thing could have possibly worked to reduce his inevitable punishment. But he was pleased that at least he got the other two out of trouble this once instead of the other way around, like usual.

While Ms. Meli was quickly preparing the day's lesson, Lily passed a note to Leo. He opened it and read *It was my fault that this happened. One day I will return the favor.* Leo looked over at Lily, and she nodded solemnly in thanks.

"All right class, now that we've got all that excitement out of the way, it's time for today's history lesson. But first, we're going to do a quick pop quiz. Everyone can thank Leo for that one."

Ms. Meli did not even bother to hide the upward curling of her smile. The whole class gave a collective sigh, the animosity almost palpable in the air.

"Let's have the man of the hour go first, shall we? Leo, what was the cause of the Great Calamity, and what was its direct result?"

Thankful that history was one of his best subjects, Leo stood up and recited his answer almost verbatim from one of his old books he had read many years ago.

"Though many of the external records from that time were lost, internal Tessera records show that, some time near the middle of the twenty-first century, abrupt climate anomalies caused massive droughts throughout much of the developed world.

"Although it was a huge blow to all of humanity, some good initially did come from it. Having a deadly common enemy proved to be just what the world needed at that time. The new technological advancements and the newly formed World Council, a direct result of the world-wide devastation, helped to unify the world and hold off total starvation and collapse. Like with most things, no system is ever perfect."

"How so, in this case?" Ms. Meli said.

"Sadly," Leo said, "one country thought they could use this opportunity to usurp the world governing body's power and try to gain dominance of all world affairs. In order to do this, its scientists developed a way to genetically modify crops to be able to grow in almost any condition.

"With this new technology dubbed the "miracle crop," that country brought an end to the Great Calamity. But, as with most new, untested technologies, there were unintended consequences. After only a few years of prosperity, the now-exclusively used miracle crop suffered a mass genetic mutation and became unable to reproduce, causing what was later recorded as the "Final Blight." Thus the world was yet again thrown into chaos. Without the miracle crop and with little food stores from the previous calamity, there was only one inevitable outcome.

"War ripped through every country, large and small, destroying everything in its wake. The only ones who could manage to survive the "Final War," as it would become known, were some of the world's largest and most powerful organizations and corporations of the era. They managed to survive by constructing large facilities underground and in some of the most remote parts of the world, one of which is where we all reside."

Leo sat down, thoroughly confident in his detailed answer.

"As always, your answer was A+ material, Leo," Ms. Meli said, "but you did gloss over one small detail. It is true we live comfortably within this facility, but in truth, many still live in the outside world. Our most recent estimates put the surviving population at about 10 percent of its peak prewar estimate, meaning we are not the only survivors. Many poor, misguided souls still reside in the wastelands and the slums of the old world, clinging to their false gods and idols."

Suddenly straightening herself as if she were a soldier at attention, she spoke in a loud clear voice. "Our sole mission as members of the great organization Tessera is to rescue those poor souls and bring about a new, perfect, just world. For we are the ones chosen to lead the world anew."

As she was proclaiming the mission statement of Tessera, the rest of the students looked on in wonderment. If one were to hear such grand ideas for long enough, one was bound to believe them eventually.

This was how it was for each person who grew up and lived in the facility. From the moment of their birth, they had all been told that they were special, that they would be critical in leading the way for the rest of humanity, that they were better, superior to the rest who dwelled outside.

Leo could understand where their sense of superiority came from, and to be totally honest, it wasn't totally unearned. Tessera was easily the largest, most advanced, and most powerful entity remaining on the planet. Sure, there were a few other contenders, but none could be called a match for Tessera in this day and age.

Leo remembered something he had once read in one of the hidden volumes within the trio's secret base. The passage detailed the early days of battle between the corporations that remained after the Final War.

Tessera came out on top against one of its major rivals at the time, Penrose Industries, and now held a monopoly on most of the world's remaining resources. The facility he was living in was built on the very prize won from that decisive battle all those years ago.

• • •

Locke's jaw tensed as he became irritated by their teacher's proclamation, for he knew that preaching such nonsense was just a front for gaining more power.

Unlike himself, who wished nothing more than to live a quiet life with his friends, all those around him constantly desired for more and more. As one who had little sense of personal greed, it was one of the few aspects of humanity he did not fully grasp.

Touted by his two friends as being the most socially perceptive and skilled in communication, in reality, he truly knew very little of what swayed the hearts of others. Hence his quiet demeanor. It was not because he hated to talk. Actually, that was far from it, but he made himself distant and reserved to be able to more closely study those around him.

Acting as if he was a spectator watching a sports game from afar, Locke's dream was to fully comprehend what drove the actions of those around him. He felt if he could finally grasp it, all his other nagging questions would fall smoothly into place.

Unlike the girl next to him, who was obsessed with what she could make with her hands, his interests were more on the intangible side. Although he, Leo, and Lily were as different as three people could be, he felt a powerful connection between them. Never having a true blood family, he mused that this must be what the bond of being a part of a family was like.

"Locke . . . Locke! It's your turn for the quiz. Stand up and answer your question." Startled from his train of thought, he returned to the tangible world. As he stood up, Locke quickly glanced at Leo and then at Lily. A faint smile briefly crossed his lips as he began to answer his question.

3

THE UNPRECEDENTED CELEBRATION

ALTHOUGH THEIR SCHOOL DAY was cut short, Leo, Locke, and Lily were already equally exhausted. Dragging themselves out of the classroom, all the other students happily rushed past them. The buzz of excitement was heavy in the air as the students talked among themselves about what treats were awaiting them.

Normally the others would be groaning at the end of the school day just like the three friends. As they got closer to their graduation, most days after school each student would do assigned tasks for their apprenticeships. It was the norm for every student in the academy to be chosen to become an apprentice for a specific type of field within the facility as they got closer to their graduation.

The students were picked for their overall aptitudes in certain areas, as well as being personally selected by specific members of the different branches of the facility.

Within the trio's class, many of the students were placed in either the military command or high-science apprenticeships, the rarest and most sought-after positions within the entire facility.

This was not the norm, but the trio's current class was the pride and joy of the entire academy, a once-in-a-generation group of students, with Leo, Lily, and Locke as its core.

Finally reaching the hallway after substantial effort, a shrill voice could be heard coming from behind them.

"*Leo!* Don't forget to go see the colonel for your punishment before the celebration begins!" Leo grimaced at Ms. Meli's statement. He had hoped she had forgotten about it, but it seemed he was not that lucky.

Leo turned to the two at his flanks. "You guys have things you need to do for the celebration, right? So, I'll just go see him now, and we can meet up afterward at the party."

They both nodded in agreement, but then Lily spoke up in a soft but cheerful voice. "Well . . . Can we at least walk with you to the command center? I need to go to the supply room near there anyways to get one of my babies. I was asked to get it to help set up for the party."

"Sure, if you guys want to, I have no objection," Leo said.

Although it didn't show on his face, he felt a little relieved that they would walk with him. Walking alone to the command center would only have sent his nerves even higher, without even factoring the colonel into the equation.

As they walked down the corridor, it was much less crowded than it had been earlier in the day. So much so, the three could easily walk side by side instead of the normal bobbing and weaving they were so used to.

Due to the festivities later, most of the workers were likely already relaxing in their personal rooms or in one of the facility's large recreational areas. As they passed one such area, they couldn't help but peek through the windows.

They could see people enjoying the swimming pool, fitness center, and even a movie theater. Leo looked on in envy, wishing that he could join them.

"After all this work is over and we finally graduate we should all take a vacation..." Locke said, with a heavy sigh, eyes fixed on the swimming pool in the distance. "I think we deserve it." The other two agreed wholeheartedly.

"I would love for you to teach me to swim," Leo said, giving Locke a slight nudge with his shoulder. Both looked at each other and laughed. They both knew very well that Locke loved the idea of water but was actually a terrible swimmer.

"Only if Lily can teach me how to make an automated swimsuit!" Locke said while glancing over at Lily.

"Don't even worry about it. That would be easy-peasy for someone like me." She grinned and flexed her bicep.

Their laughter echoed throughout the empty corridor. What made the whole thing funnier for Leo was, now that the idea had been planted, Lily would undoubtedly try to make one sooner rather than later.

Finally, having made it past the torture of watching other people have fun, they approached the command center's large, intimidating steel doors. As they approached, the lone soldier standing guard glared down at them, appearing to size them up.

Locke and Lily gave Leo a sympathetic nod as they continued past him, averting their faces from the piercing eyes of the guard.

The guard's sharp voice rang out. "State your business. Who are you here for?"

Leo reflexively straightened himself and said in an equally loud, clear voice, "I was told by Ms. Meli in the academy to speak to the colonel for punishment."

The guard examined him closely, seeming to judge whether what he said was true or not. Leo felt as though he was nothing more than a pane of glass before this man. He felt as though it would be impossible to hide anything, whether it be physical or not, from his scrutinous gaze. After a moment of silence that to Leo felt like minutes of bated breath, the guard's face finally softened.

"Aye, the colonel has been expecting you. You can go right in. His office is down the hall to the left."

Leo internally breathed a sigh of relief.

This man . . . he thought to himself. *No wonder why he's the guard for the command center. I can't imagine anyone getting anything past this guy.*

As he stepped through the doorway, the guard said, "Whatever you do, don't make him any angrier, because I'll be the one who has to deal with the aftermath." Though he was giving Leo sound advice, his demeanor was menacing, as he held his rifle. "Then I'll have to be the one who has to find and punish you."

The guard kept a perfectly straight face, so it was hard for Leo to determine if it was meant in a threatening or half-joking way.

Leo just nodded as the door closed behind him with a loud hiss. Taking the man's words to heart he walked down the corridor.

• • •

Leo passed many people in high-ranking military uniforms; each one looked busier than the last, even on a day of celebration like this. He admired their work ethic, however the military could rarely take holidays. For the day that one became lazy was the day that one died in time of war. Although they were not currently engaged in war, the threat of war and sabotage constantly loomed, and there were many who wished for Tessera to be destroyed.

The ones on top will always be targeted by those beneath them, Leo thought, as he approached the office door.

After checking himself thoroughly to make sure he looked presentable, Leo quickly but firmly knocked on the door. Almost instantly, he heard "Permission to enter," and the door opened before Leo.

Moving with the swiftness and grace of a seasoned veteran, Leo entered, stood at attention, and gave a crisp military salute.

Although he was not officially in the military yet, this was the standard greeting to one's superior within the facility. That was just how much power the military branch possessed. Still at attention, Leo looked at his surroundings. He had never been in this office before, and his curiosity took over.

It was a larger room than he had expected. It contained two large couches with a table between them, a large map table off to one side, a cabinet filled with military-related items on the other, and a grand desk, where the colonel sat in a high-backed chair.

Everything in the room was in pristine condition which would be expected in an office of a high-ranking military officer. However, there was one thing that transfixed Leo so much that he lowered his salute.

Directly behind the desk, affixed to the wall, was the head of a large creature. It was an animal, with imposing fangs, that Leo had never seen before, its expression frozen in perpetual pain. Leo gazed at the unsettling sight as he imagined what that animal must have looked like in its prime and the events that led it to be currently residing on the wall of the colonel.

"Who said 'at ease,' soldier!"

Breaking his salute without permission from the colonel was a grave display of disrespect.

"Even though you are top of your class, you may still need harsher training yet, *boy*." The colonel scowled at him and then stood up.

"You . . . who came here for punishment are foolish enough to crave more punishment? All right then, I will oblige you."

The colonel walked around his desk and stood mere inches from Leo. Their height difference was substantial, and Leo strained his neck to keep eye contact with him.

Suddenly stars appeared in his eyes, and all he could process was the hardness of the ground pressing against his cheek.

"That was for the blatant disrespect of a superior officer," the colonel spat, his fist still held at the stomach height of where Leo once stood. As the rest of Leo's senses caught up with his body, he felt an extraordinary pain radiating from his abdomen.

"Though we have never met before, I know much about you. I know that personal pain will not help to further train you. Hence, I have decided to instead transfer the rest of your punishment to your two companions."

Leo finally managed to fight the pain for a moment as he looked up to see the faintest smile spreading across the colonel's face.

"It is always the subordinates who are impacted by the actions of their superiors, whether those choices lead to victory or certain death. A true leader must always consider such things."

Lowering himself to Leo, he looked directly into his eyes. Leo could feel the colonel's piercing blue eyes burrowing deep into his soul. Having seemed to come to some sort of decision, he stood back up and swiftly kicked Leo, who was still doubled up in pain.

"The world is not a fair and just place. I still see much that needs to be worked out of you, one way or another, before you can become what the director says you're destined to become. We'll see if you can live up to that number one stitched on your shoulder, although I have my doubts."

The colonel sneered one last time as he stepped on Leo's trembling body as he crossed the room.

Hearing the cold mechanical hiss of the door open and then close, Leo finally managed to let out a faint guttural sound of pain and anger. It sounded like the cry of some injured wild animal.

Of course, Leo was angry at the colonel, but mostly his current anger was directed towards his own shortcomings. The words spoken by that man repeated in his hazy, pain-filled mind as he lay there clutching his abdomen.

After an ambiguous amount of time had passed, the door reopened, but from the footsteps, it was clear that they belonged to a different individual. Feeling a strong hand pull him up by the arm, Leo looked at the man helping him to his feet. It was the guard with the hawklike eyes from before. Giving Leo the slightest expression of sympathy, he pulled him upright.

"I thought something had happened after seeing the colonel storm out, and then you were nowhere to be seen."

Holding Leo steady, he guided him out the door as he spoke in an almost apologetic tone. "The colonel's lessons may be a bit harsh, but he truly means well by them." The guard said this without looking at Leo. "I can say from personal experience they work extremely well."

Leo, only capable of nodding his head, fully understood what the guard was implying. "Just don't tell anyone that I helped you;

if word got out that I was so softhearted I might experience getting 'retrained' as well."

Again, Leo was unsure if the man was serious or half-joking as he and the guard reached the exit of the command center. Finally, able to stand on his own power, Leo thankfully saluted the man, who silently returned the motion as they parted ways.

Leo slowly made his way down one of the many corridors towards one of the large dining hall areas in the facility. Locke and Lily should be there already, preparing for the Founding Celebration later that day.

Still grimacing from the pain, Leo silently wished he could have thanked the guard more; it was indeed rare to find such a kind soldier within the facility. Although what the guard did wasn't really all that much, just the simple act of compassion he had shown was enough for Leo. Realizing that he would most likely never meet the man again, Leo decided to seek him out and be sure to thank him properly. *I never even got his name.*

Mentally kicking himself for yet another mistake, Leo reached the dining hall. Compared to its normal, rather plain interior, it now looked as though someone had set off a bomb filled with bright colors and festive decorations.

Just then, Lily came bounding over to his side with what appeared to be an actual bomb in one of her hands.

"LE—" Before she could finish calling out to him, Leo had already cut her off, his voice was full of both curiosity and fear . . .

"What on earth are you holding???"

"Oh, this?" she said, as she parked herself right in front of Leo and casually waved the object around. "It's a paint bomb I made. The party coordinator said I could paint the walls anyway I wanted to." She gave a mischievous grin.

It was obvious to Leo that Lily had taken some liberties when it came to "any way you want." *Typical Lily*, he thought to himself and shook his head.

Leo sighed. "I don't think that's what they meant but oh well."

As Lily turned to point at the walls, currently covered in multicolored paint, Leo had to admit it looked rather nice.

While they were busy admiring Lily's handiwork, Leo spotted Locke farther into the room. He was guiding a large, human-like robot, which was hauling massive tables into position. Lily grabbed Leo's arm and pulled him towards Locke's position.

"How's the ECLP-112 running? I just modified it the other day," she called out to Locke.

He turned with an annoyed look on his face. "This thing is a pain to control! You need to consider other people when you make this kind of thing! The controls are so complex. Not everyone can be as smart as you when it comes to machines. Do you want me to give you more lessons about dealing with other people??"

Hearing Locke's criticism, Lily's expression changed from one of happiness to gloom. Nothing could change her mood faster than someone criticizing one of her prized creations, especially Locke.

Within the three's dynamic, Leo was always the one who complimented her works wholeheartedly, while Locke, who could be called slightly technologically challenged, was the one to interject some criticism and practical concern into his reactions to her designs. Normally this devolved into Lily and Locke exchanging rather well-thought-out verbal jabs or childish insults.

Perhaps not wanting to get into a verbal brawl in the middle of the mess hall, Locke quickly changed the subject. "Leo,

I noticed you limping as you walked over here. Did something happen?" Locke said, trying his best to steer the conversation. Unfortunately, Leo's face couldn't help but wrinkle as he remembered what had happened not that long ago.

"Well, I made the colonel mad and he had to . . . retrain me, if you get my drift."

Leo's subconsciously grabbed his abdomen as he continued. "He told me that my actions have consequences, and that they not only affect me but everyone around me, as well."

Locke nodded. "So, he is not only going to punish you but all of us as well? Honestly, I can't argue with that train of thought."

Lily, who had quickly recovered from her gloominess, began to fidget in place. "Explain it better; I don't get it. Not everyone can be as smart as you when it comes to the things people say."

All three of them cracked a smile and began to laugh.

"But seriously," Leo said, "be careful you guys. The colonel is brutal. I don't want you to suffer like I just had to. So be sure to not do anything to make yourself stick out."

Trying to lighten the suddenly depressing mood, Lily spoke up in a rather cheerful manner. "Don't worry about us; we're tougher than we look. Besides, three are always tougher than one, so how could he possibly beat us?"

Dumbstruck by her tenacious words, Leo and Locke could only manage to stare at her. *What a girl*, Leo thought. To have the gall to even jest about standing up against one of the most terrifying and powerful men in all the facility was almost unthinkable. The worst part was that he had a feeling that she was more than half-serious.

Interrupting the silence was the sound of a loud voice coming from the front of the hall. Without Leo realizing it, the once nearly empty room had quickly filled with people.

"Attention everyone! Everything is ready, and so the time has arrived. Let the festivities begin!" The loud voice rang throughout the hall, and in response, an even louder cheer rose from those gathered.

All at once, there was a mad scramble. Those who were standing near the hall's entrance all rushed in at once. Their destination was the area where Locke had been carefully laying out the food and the tables just a few moments before. Exactly where the three had the misfortune of currently standing.

As if the waves were breaking onto the shore, the mass of people slammed into the unsuspecting trio. Used to being entangled in large crowds, Leo, Lily, and Locke grabbed hold of each other and just barely pulled themselves out of the rip current that was the undulating mass of hungry wild animals.

"I had a feeling this was going to happen, so I, um, 'misplaced' some of the food trays and left them over there." Barely managing to get the words out, Locke pointed to the far side of the room, where three trays full of assorted delicious food items remained untouched.

Finally breaking away from the throng of ravenous individuals, the trio turned to each other and broke out into another fit of laughter. "You really saved us this time," Lily said. "I thought I was going to drown. Even worse, all the good food would be gone!"

Picking up the trays, they walked past many tables full of different groups of Tessera members while they looked for a place to gorge themselves. Though there was no assigned seating, individuals seemed to seek out and self-segregate with those in their own group. Continuing to look for a place to sit with people that they recognized, they passed many large groups from the various divisions throughout the facility.

The largest and by far the rowdiest was the military division, specifically the tables full of the average grunt soldier. As they passed by the soldiers' tables, Leo searched for the guard from earlier, but to no avail. He must have been still on duty. Leo noticed many of the soldiers shooting glances of silent judgment towards them.

The military officers had a grand table all to themselves at the front of the hall and were being much more civil than the grunts.

The second-largest group was the science division, which was broken up into many subsections. But as a whole, they tended to all get along and mix rather well, as opposed to the soldiers.

In the meantime, a middle-aged man in a lab coat waved cheerfully to the trio as they passed by. "Happy Founding Celebration you three! Don't eat too much cake, you hear? Or you'll be seeing me again before you know it!"

The man in question was from the science division, but more specifically, he was one of the heads of the medical division, the eccentric Doctor Jacobs.

"Thank you for always looking out for us, Dr. Jacobs, but we are not kids anymore! We won't come crying to you just because we have some cuts and bruises," Lily said, trying her best to act more adult-like, while at the same time failing miserably to avert her reddening cheeks.

The doctor raised his hands defensively in the air. He replied with the smile of a true medical professional, albeit with some minor screws loose. "Ok, ok, I understand. You guys are officially not children anymore. But in my book, you guys will always be my little experim—ahem—patients."

After the science division, were tables full of the staff from the academy, including all their teachers, all except Ms. Meli, who was surprisingly nowhere to be seen. Leo breathed a sigh of relief as they hurried past those particular tables.

The second-to-last group was made up of the various craftsmen and maintenance workers. As opposed to the other tables, many politely nodded to the three as they passed.

The students from the academy sat at the last table. Though it was by far the smallest group, it had the largest variety of members of all shapes and sizes. On one end of the table sat the newest cadets, all of whom were around the ripe age of five years old. But as one went farther down the table, the ages steadily progressed up until about sixteen.

Picking an empty spot two-thirds down the table, the three sat down with their large trays of food.

Luke stood up and enthusiastically pointed to the small mountains of food the trio had brought. *"Where did you guys get all of that?!??"*

In comparison, the food on the plates of the students around them looked as though they only managed to scrape together the less appealing leftovers from the initial feeding frenzy.

Unfortunately, that was the hierarchy of the facility. Those who were weakest were always at the bottom. If they wanted to change that, they would have to force themselves to the top by sheer effort, willpower, and skill to earn respect and status.

Finally beginning to chip away at his pile of food, Leo could see the longing and slight jealousy in the expressions of those around them. Leo turned to Locke, and their eyes met for only a moment. However, that was all it took for Locke to understand Leo's intentions, and he gave the smallest nod of approval while patting the back of the now-coughing Lily, who clenched both her fists.

Putting down his fork, Leo pushed his tray, with a rather large sigh, towards the middle of the table. "I guess we can share with you guys. It's not like we could finish this much anyways, and besides, if we kept it all to ourselves, Lily would probably choke to death."

Before his fingers had even left the tray, more than half of the food had already vanished. The rather sly children had all seemingly been expecting this outcome all along.

As the sounds of chewing became a dull roar, two small children no older than seven timidly approached the seated trio, hand in hand.

"W-we-we just wanted to say thank you for the food. My sister and I think it's nice that you always do such kind things for us, and yet no one ever thanks you guys." Speaking with overlapping voices the two shyly thanked them.

"Don't worry about it, Taylor . . . Tyler," Leo said, turning to each of the downcast children. "It means a lot that you two care so much, but you need to be careful. If the higher-ups see you acting in such a way, it will only lead to trouble for the two of you, and that's the last thing I want to see happen to the cutest pair of twins in the facility."

Leo ruffled the heads of the two, and their faces instantly turned red, and they began to squirm from embarrassment. It was true that no one ever thanked the trio for their kind deeds, but it was the norm in the facility such as this one. Pointless things such as kindness and compassion were only tools meant to be used by the strong. The weak had no right to such luxury, or so taught Tessera.

To openly show appreciation for kindness from one stronger than one's self would only lead to punishment. The mantra of Tessera dictated that one who wants to be kind must first become strong, and to become truly strong it must be done alone. A chain is only as strong as its weakest link, and Tessera was a strong chain indeed.

Interrupting the sentimental moment, the brash Luke stormed over to Locke, his hands raised in front of himself as if holding an invisible plate and standing uncomfortably close.

"If you're going to be so nice to them, you might as well give me what I'm owed!! I didn't forget! You still owe me an extra piece of cake! You thought I would forget, but I *didn'ttt!!!*"

It was obvious to everyone but Luke that Locke, who loved his peace and quiet, was positively vexed at the situation.

"I'll give it to you when they hand it out. Uh, can't you see that no one has any yet?"

The animosity could be felt coming off Locke's breath as he spoke, trying his best to ignore Luke's existence, which was oppressively close to his own.

"I just don't want to be cheated; I know you always trick me, but not this time! I'm gonna sit right here until they give them out."

Locke looked to his left. "Lily, switch places with me. If I have to keep listening to this, I think I'll have to shove the cake down his throat just to get some peace and quiet."

Barely listening to Locke as she continued to eat an amazing amount of food for her rather small size, she nodded and the two switched places. Just as Locke was finally able to start tuning out the sounds of conversations around him and begin to eat, a loud, booming voice drowned out all others.

"Ahem! Before we come to the end of tonight's festivities, it is time for the director to say a few words."

The voice came from a serious-looking woman standing at a podium on the stage at the front of the dining hall. Next to her stood the director, the colonel, and a few other department heads, who looked very pleased with themselves as they looked out over the densely packed crowd.

The director walked to the podium. "First and foremost, I would like to thank all of you for all the hard work you've done this year. It has been one of the most prosperous in recent memory.

"It has recently been confirmed that our sister facility in the south has finally gained complete control over the entire southern region and its vast oil reserve, with the help of our forces to the west. The next operation of the combined southern and western forces is to join with us here.

"Though our territory is much larger, we must show our resolve and finally drive out the dangerous elements from our own region. Penrose Industries has never recovered from their embarrassing defeat all those years ago, and K-141 can only be described as a ragtag group of mercenary guerrillas with no brains. The only true threat to our hold on the region is the various religious zealots hidden throughout the Wasteland, gaining power and causing chaos even as we speak.

"The weak refugees and mindset of the old world must be brought to light. Tessera's dream of a newer, better . . . a perfect world is almost at hand! At last, we hold over three-fifths of all inhabitable territory, and with the assistance from the southern and western coalition forces, these eastern lands will finally belong to us!"

He reached out his hand as if to help someone. Thunderous applause filled the room.

"Thank you, thank you. The future is bright indeed, especially since Tessera now holds a trump card. I would like to call up our three important guests to the stage."

There was a murmur of confusion throughout the crowd.

Trying to act as though it was the most normal thing in the world, Leo rose from his seat, followed by Lily, and lastly by Locke. They walked towards the stage, taking a flanking position by the director.

Leo could hear many small noises of surprise and confusion from his position on the stage, as they stood overlooking the small sea of people.

Raising his hands, the director skillfully silenced the clamor of the crowd. "I know many of you are confused by my bringing these students up here before you. Many of you may already be familiar with these three. But now that the gestation period is concluded, I can finally reveal to you all here one of Tessera's greatest successes to date."

He motioned to the trio.

"I would like to formally introduce to you these three amazing children. They have broken all documented Tessera records and have progressed faster than any other academy candidates to date. They are the newest hope for this utterly ravaged world. They will be the stepping-stones, models for all future humans to strive to emulate. As Tessera's Three Pillars, they will help to guide the world anew."

At his words, a deafening roar erupted from the crowd. As they stood on the stage it was impossible to tell what was being said, but the mood seemed to be split. The air around the science division seemed to be an excited one, while the military seemed the loudest and most skeptical. The other divisions seemed almost unfazed.

After a few moments, Colonel Veers was the one to raise his hand this time. The room instantaneously went from a deafening roar to being able to hear a pin hitting the ground.

"I know many of you are confused over what has just been said, but first we shall let Director Anderson explain himself, and you all will be sure to listen well." As he spoke, he glared at the tables full of rowdy military personnel.

"My thanks, Colonel Veers," the director said. "You are as effective as ever. To fully explain why these children are standing beside me, I need to tell you all about one of the most top secret and crucial programs to Tessera for many years now. Its sole purpose was to raise advanced humans; one could even say we strove for human perfection.

"Although their dream eluded them for many years, the members of this secret project finally were able to reach a form of success. These three children before you are the fruits of their years of labor and dedication. We waited until now to make this public because we were evaluating each of them to be undoubtedly sure that they were what we had envisioned. And I dare say we have surpassed our goal. Each of these children has advanced at a rate never before seen in all aspects of human development. With these three, the Three Pillars of Tess—"

. . .

An ear-piercing squealing sound, followed by a tremendous crash caused the whole room to reflexively recoil at the sudden noise. The disciplined soldiers present were the first to recover from their surprise. They were quick to scan their surroundings to pinpoint the possible threat.

The colonel had recovered instantly and already held his pistol in his steady hand as his eyes scanned his surroundings like a hawk looking for his prey.

Like a small animal, Leo's eyes were fixed on the most powerful predator in the room. Having gone from startled to completely calm and in control in a blink of an eye, Leo was more than slightly impressed.

Noticing the colonel's gaze had become fixed, Leo followed his line of sight to the source of the loud disturbance. Slightly beyond the edges of the crowd, there were pieces of what was once a rather large humanoid robot.

From the stage, marks on the ground could be seen, and they look very much like tire skid marks that, when followed, led right to the remains of the robot. That explained the squealing sound, but the crash, on the other hand, was a bit more difficult to comprehend.

From first impressions, it seemed as if the robot was driven at full speed towards the tables that had only just recently been laid with desserts and crashed unceremoniously into them.

As Leo quickly began to piece together what had happened, he turned to Lily and quietly said, "Did you actually add them to it???"

Lily stared at her feet and gave a slight nod.

Leo clicked his tongue. Lily, who had been asked by the research and development division to create the large robot for the purpose of "moving cumbersome items," had made what she liked to call "necessary improvements" to its design over time.

One such design improvement that she envisioned was adding rocket boosters to the feet of the robot. "What if it needs to jump over or reach something that's really, really tall??" she had said.

Although she was undoubtedly a genius, her sense of design utility could use some slight realignment. So, with this new information, the scene before Leo became all too clear. Unlike if it had plowed straight into the tables, the majority of the robot's pieces were scattered in such a way that it looked as though it was dropped from the ceiling and, upon hitting the floor, exploded in all directions from the impact.

To the average onlooker that would almost seem impossible since it was standing in the corner of the room only moments before. But when you factor in the secret additions to its design, it was painfully clear that it had gone out of control somehow and was on a fated path to collide with the tables. Somehow the boosters were triggered in a last-ditch effort to avoid a certain collision. It seemed that the idea was much better in theory than in actual execution.

As some sense of order returned to the crowd, the colonel holstered his weapon, stepped up to the podium, and began to speak. "I do not know if this was an accident or purposely orchestrated by a person or persons unknown. But let me say this . . . For disrupting this joyous celebration and even having the audacity to interrupt Director Anderson, I will *personally* investigate and determine who is responsible."

Although speaking in a calm and collected manner, it was

crystal clear to Leo that the colonel, now clenching his jaw, was beyond furious. Slowly clenching and opening his jaw he continued.

"If those responsible have the sense to reveal themselves now, I will promise to consider leniency. However, if I must be forced to smoke you out, this affront will be your last . . . No matter your standing or intentions, your judgment will be swift and eternal. I swear this on the duty of my station."

Leo's mind began to race as he grasped the implications that were just made. Locke nudged him and, shrugging his shoulders, mouthed the words *Where is Lily??"*

Mimicking what Locke had just done, Leo looked in every possible direction and then settled on a small door directly off the stage's flank that led to the kitchens. Moving his hand slightly, Leo subtly motioned to the door. Locke gave a slight nod of understanding. Trying his best to keep his expression straight as he glanced at the door, Leo was dumbfounded. *She ran away?????*

4

AN UNEXPECTED DISCOVERY

FOLLOWING THE STREAM OF PEOPLE exiting the hall, Leo and Locke finally managed to take a deep breath. They had been holding it the whole time they stood next to the colonel. Thankfully, he had been barking his orders for everyone to leave immediately to begin his investigation. So, using his order as an excuse, the two had immediately rushed off the stage.

Leo knew that Locke had most likely prepared a decent-enough lie to give as an answer if anyone were to ask the location of the last member of their trio. Thankfully, it seemed no one had noticed the absence of their third member amid the mass exodus from the hall.

As Leo turned to Locke in the throng of the loud crowd, Locke read Leo's worried expression perfectly. Shrugging his shoulders, Locke sighed and said, "Honestly, if anyone asked, I would have just said she really had to go to the bathroom or something. I really hope she just had a stomachache and went back to her room . . . but I have a strong feeling that isn't the case."

Leo sighed and summarized what he had figured out about the strange incident that had just occurred. "So, most likely Lily is feeling responsible for what happened. You know how she gets when something like this happens. Anything to do with her 'babies' and she loses all sense of reason."

Thinking back, Leo remembered an instance when Lily had hidden away for over a week. She had been so distraught, that no one was able to find her unless it was at a mealtime.

In that one case, one of her smaller robots, which happen to look quite like a small rodent, was discovered inside her school desk. The teacher let out a flurry of high-pitched screams as she smashed it into a million pieces with a textbook right in front of Lily.

To Lily, each one of her inventions, no matter the size or complexity, was a piece of her identity. Lily was like a mother with her children. Unlike Locke, who had no idea what that was like, since he couldn't remember his own parents, Leo understood Lily's feelings very well. He sometimes felt as though he were the elder brother of the three even though they were all around the same age. Like Lily, who was proud of her inventions, Leo felt a similar pride for his two closest friends.

The crowd thinned as they made their way back towards the living quarters. Instead of the unrelenting mixture of voices, individual conversations could start to be heard from those walking with them. Trying to subtly eavesdrop, Leo could make out bits and pieces here and there. The feeling among those in their general vicinity was a mixture of fear with some tinges of dark humor.

Some were afraid that there was a possible spy in the facility. Others were making rather crude jokes about what would happen when the colonel got his hands on whomever was responsible, spy or not. Overhearing that kind of talk only raised Leo's anxiety. He knew that if they pinned this on Lily, there was no way it would end well.

Reaching Lily's room, Leo opened the door and prayed she would be inside. Announcing their entry and stepping inside, their fears were realized, as she was nowhere to be found. They checked any possible hiding spots she might have had. As Leo quickly paced back and forth in the middle of the room, Locke quietly sat in Lily's desk chair.

"How did the robot manage to go out of control in the first place??" Locke said. "I was the only one using it earlier, and it was working perfectly."

Leo stopped his pacing. "From the skid patterns it looked as though someone was steering it, but then it somehow lost control. They then, either purposely or by accident, hit the rocket boosters to try to evade at the last second. I doubt they had ever used any kind of control system like that before."

"Yeah, that's very possible. That thing was definitely tricky to use. The controller is crazy complicated . . . Wait a second . . ."

As Locke's face wrinkled in thought he patted himself down as if searching for something. "Where is the remote?" he said. "I know I had it . . . I never gave it back to Lily, who was supposed to give it back to the maintenance crew after the party."

"You probably either dropped it and someone hit it accidentally, or it was stolen for some reason."

Covering his face with his hand, Locke nodded in agreement. "I hope I just dropped it, and someone stepped on it or something, because if someone stole it . . . I don't even wanna think about it . . ."

Leo held out his hand to the slumped Locke. "We should go back inside the dining hall and see if we can find it before the investigators do; maybe we can clear all this up without anyone getting into trouble."

Finally managing to raise his head, Locke reached up and took hold of Leo's hand. He didn't show it externally at first, but he couldn't help but wearily chastise himself.

"How many times have we been in almost this exact situation before? What would I do if you weren't always there to pull me back up?" A bittersweet expression formed on his face as he got to his feet.

"Don't worry about it," Leo said. "Come on." He dragged Locke out the door like a child. They retraced their path all the way back to the entrance of the dining hall. Unlike the last time, it was eerily quiet and deserted as they cautiously approached the large entrance. As they were about to enter, they heard faint voices from deeper inside.

Holding his hand out to block Locke from moving inside, Leo strained to hear and decipher the jumbled voices coming from inside the room.

"The colonel . . ."

"Pissed off this time . . . He even . . . Kyle was devastated."

"Looking through all this crap . . ."

"I hope I find whoever did . . ."

"Yo, Sarge, what's this controller thing?"

Leo could only pick up bits and pieces of the conversations going on in the room, but he felt they should not go inside, or they faced being picked apart by the group of disgruntled soldiers.

"Shh . . . Be quiet. It sounds like one of them found something," Locke whispered to Leo.

Hey, don't tell me to be quiet when your breathing is so damn loud,

Leo thought to himself as he inched away from Locke, who had managed to put his mouth a little too close for comfort to Leo's ear. Moving back, he stepped on Locke's right foot, who squealed in pain. Startled, Leo fell backward, creating an even more noticeable racket.

"What was that?!?!? It sounded like a pig squealing or something. Let's go check it out. It came from the hallway."

Leo and Locke, hearing the voices from inside, looked at each other in panic. Leo quickly got back to his feet. As if he were Locke's shadow, he followed closely behind Locke as they sprinted down the hallway and around the next corner.

Falling to their knees the moment they rounded the corner, both struggled to get their ragged breathing under control. Straining to hear over the thumping in his chest, it seemed to Leo that they had not been discovered.

"I don't see anything. It was probably just some kids running in the hall. What else could have made that awful sound, other than some stupid kids . . . Or maybe your wife? Heh-heh-heh."

"Hey! What was that for?"

"What? You know it's true."

Hearing the banter of the retreating soldiers, Leo finally managed to get his heartbeat under control.

"Well, that was a close one," Leo said. "Better that we didn't get involved. I think one of them found the remote. That's what it sounded like, at least.

"If the person responsible left the evidence behind, they most likely weren't a spy. They wouldn't want to leave evidence like that laying out in the open. It's more likely that it was an accident, and they just dropped it and ran after the commotion."

Locke shook his head. "I don't think so. If it was me, I would want those hunting for me to believe it was just an accident. I also wouldn't want to be carrying any evidence of the deed on my person while walking past all those guards at the exit. If it would have been me, I might have planted it on a dupe just to avert suspicion and cause a little more confusion."

"Well not everyone thinks the same way as you do, that's for sure." Leo was all too familiar with Locke's special way of thinking. Even though he did not necessarily approve of his methods, he always helped to give a different point of view. Leo playfully jabbed at Locke. "Man, I would be terrified if you one day chose to use your powers for evil."

Locke didn't let it show on his face, but Leo's banter made him genuinely happy.

"Well, so long as I have you and Lily, I don't think that would be a problem," Locke said. "I know you guys will keep me on the straight and narrow."

He gave Leo a faint smile, and they continued down the hall, in a much calmer fashion than moments before.

Repeating themselves from earlier that morning, they made their way past the command center, into the supply closet, through the cramped duct system, and finally dropped into their secret base.

This was the only possible place Lily could be hiding. However, unlike earlier in the day, they were not greeted by their trusty robotic canine companion. That surprised Leo, who had preemptively braced himself to be taken down to the ground at any moment by the overly excited Rusty.

As Leo called out into the dark depth of the room, no response was heard from either Rusty or Lily. "Where could he be? Rusty! Here boy!"

"Huh. Maybe he's charging or something?"

It was possible but Leo had an ominous feeling that seemed to be amplified by the oppressive darkness of the room.

They began to search the room, calling out for both Lily and Rusty. They made sure to look between each tower of boxes as they carefully navigated their way through the pathways overrun by the sheer amount of clutter. Finally reaching the room's farthest point from the entrance, they spotted a faint light emanating from the area around Lily's rather large workbench.

"That light wasn't on when we were here earlier; she must be here somewhere. Making sure to keep his voice low, Leo called out in a clear and projecting manner. "Lily! Come on out!"

Reaching the source of the illumination, Locke turned the dial on the lamp to its maximum setting.

Scattered all over the table were various schematics and parts for designs. Noticing one that resembled a familiar figure, Locke picked it up to get a better look.

"Look, this is the design for that humanoid robot I was using today . . . She must have been looking it over, for some reason."

Just as he tilted the page in Leo's direction, a faint rustling sound could be heard coming from what seemed like the wall beyond the table. Locke looked at Leo. "Did you hear that? How did she get inside the wall?"

Leaning forward and putting all his weight on the table, Locke pressed his ear against the cold wall. The table suddenly shifted slightly under his weight. "Leo, did you see that??"

"See what? I didn't notice anything other than that weird sound coming from the wall."

Locke pulled on the table. "The table just moved, but isn't it mounted to the wa—" The whole table and a small section of the wall moved out of place. Silently they peered inside the small opening in the wall.

A passageway led to another small space, where more faint lights cast shadows on the walls. They quietly called out again for Lily as they crouched down and made their way slowly inside the mysterious space.

It wasn't really what one would consider a room at all. It was just a rather large gap between the walls of their storage room and the adjacent room. It wasn't uncommon to have throughways or small spaces between older and newer portions of the facility. When renovations were done the extra space was normally converted to maintenance pathways or just ended up being forgotten about, like this one.

There was just enough room for Leo and Locke to stand up. What looked like a small, makeshift bed, piled high with worn blankets, was against one wall. In each of the room's corners, there were more small piles. These looked to contain things that would make for very uncomfortable and dangerous bedding.

"Weapons?" Leo said. "Are those new weapons? How did those get here?"

While Leo couldn't help walking closer to investigate, Locke sat on the corner of the mound of a bed, putting one hand to his chin and the other absentmindedly behind himself as he leaned back in thought.

"Did Lily steal all these? These definitely were not already here like those super old ones in the other room. These look almost exactly like the ones the soldiers currently use."

Almost as if reacting to the name currently under discussion, the bed Locke sat on moved just the faintest amount. With one fluid motion, Locke turned around and pushed the small mountain of blankets to the side. What suddenly appeared under the blankets was simultaneously an everyday sight for Locke and one that was very strange indeed.

What greeted him was the outline of a young sleeping girl, which one could say was very normal indeed. But entangled within her slender arms was not the body of a warm and furry dog but one made completely out of cold, unfeeling metal.

As Locke looked down at the pair, he smiled. In its own way, it was a very adorable sight.

Looking closer at the endearing sight before him, he could see faint remnants of the redness and puffiness around her still-closed eyes.

Noticing the now exposed Lily, Leo rushed to the bedside and began shaking her awake. "Hey! Wake uuup!! Where did all this stuff come from?? How long have you known about this place? Tell me you didn't steal these from the soldiers!"

Question after question poured from Leo's mouth as Lily finally began to stir. Seemingly unfazed by the torrent of questions, she slowly sat up while rubbing the grogginess from her still-red eyes.

"Huh? . . . Leo . . . Locke. What are you guys doing here?"

Still within her embrace, Rusty, who had awakened from sleep mode, was becoming antsy as he inquisitively tilted his metallic snout in each of their directions.

"First things first," Leo said. Why did you run away from the Founding Celebration?!?"

Lily began to anxiously pet the squirming Rusty within her arms. "Wellll . . . I didn't mean to run away without telling you guys . . . But after I saw what happened with my ECLP-112, I just knew I had to come here and review my blueprints; it should not have ever been able to activate in that way . . . I thought I installed a safety lock, and I was so upset at the thought of the accident somehow being my fault, my legs just took over, and I came rushing here to check."

• • •

Released from her arms, Rusty quickly jumped down and trotted over to Leo and Locke, looking up at them as if begging to be petted.

"I'll never understand why you programmed him to love being petted so much. Especially for something that can't actually feel it when you do it," Locke said but still reached down to rub Rusty's twitching metallic ears.

"I know you're always super methodical when it comes to your programming, and I am positive that your plans called for the safety to have been active, right?" Leo said.

"Yeah. I even triple checked, and the safety mechanism should have been active and prevented the firing of the boosters."

Leo sighed. "That doesn't look good then. I have a bad feeling. Maybe it was sabotaged by someone . . . Oh, also, before I forget . . . Why do you have all these weapons here?!?"

Before Lily could open her mouth, the trio heard the loud but familiar noise of a door opening, quickly followed by the muffled sounds of many feet entering, and by the closing hiss of the same door.

Turning where the sound originated from, the trio was only greeted by a blank wall. *What room is next to this?* Leo thought to himself, trying his best to remain silent in order to listen in.

"Now that everyone is present, let's get down to business. The timing of the incident that occurred earlier today is most unnerving. Is it possible that our security has been breached by outside entities?"

The trio strained their ears trying to listen to the voice. None of them recognized it. However, the voice that responded to the unfamiliar voice was one the three could never forget.

"It is a possibility; even our tightest security can be breached . . . although, it would take a great deal of skill and effort to enter this facility, then manage to roam around without being immediately discovered. Which means . . . either there is a wolf in sheep's clothing among us, or it was truly some random accident. In my expert opinion, however, I believe one of the last major players has planted a rather skilled spy in our beloved facility."

Leo's listened intently to the man whom he feared above all else.

"Director Anderson, if I can have your permission, I would like to allow some of my best men to covertly gather intelligence to discover if this theory is true. It is not my intention to circumvent the intelligence division's jurisdiction. However, for these circumstances, I think we both know the fewer people involved in this investigation the better."

"I agree with your assessment of the situation. It is in our best interest to be overly cautious. The timing seemed just too perfect for me as well, especially now that the western and southern forces are on their way here. We must uncover their goal and quickly; this must be resolved as fast as possible. This is a very sensitive time for Tessera. We must not squander our future victory."

"Yes, sir!"

Many voices suddenly rang out in unison, penetrating the wall that the three were motionlessly pressed against.

"On a side note, Dr. Jacobs, how are the final preparations coming along with those three?"

"Oh! They are almost perfect! Unlike the last few trials, these three are advancing at a much faster rate and, personalitywise, seem much more stable. I must send my thanks to the boys on the forty-seventh floor for doing such a bang-up job.

"Honestly, I'm even starting to get a little attached to them this time. Especially the one named Leo. Whatever mixture of traits they used to make him, really, it is incredible. The conditioning we use barely seems to affect him at all, unlike with the other two. Hopefully, when the final appraisal is completed, they too could be put to some use, although there's always space for new subjects on the forty-seventh floor."

Though the doctor's voice sounded as if he were joking, the director answered in a very matter-of-fact tone.

"Well, if any of them fail to meet my high expectations, then I would be happy to hand them over to you. Anything to help keep the spirits up for one of my esteemed colleagues."

"Thank you, sir. You really know how to keep us all motivated. I must find some way to show my gratitude."

Just as the director was responding to this flattery, the trio could hear the door open. A hurried voice said, "Sir, we have a report! Men stationed in the dining hall have found something. We have brought it at the request of Captain Miller to the vault on the forty-seventh floor."

"Finally, some good news, I will head there immediately."

The trio listened closely to the person they believed to be

the director as he promptly left the room, followed closely by the other occupants of the unseen room.

An enveloping silence had returned to Lily's hideout. Rusty was the first one to shatter the deafening quiet by fulfilling his rather detailed programming and scratching one of his ears with a robotic hind leg. Although he was purely mechanical, it was easy to forget that he wasn't a living, breathing dog.

Lily's voice was trembling as she turned to her two companions. "Wha-what was that? What on earth were they talking about? I could barely understand any of it."

Locke wore the same expression that Lily did, one of fear mixed with confusion. "I don't know, and I don't think we should have been listening in. If they find out that we were eavesdropping, they might think we are the spies."

"Well for one thing, we shouldn't just stay here," Leo said. "That would make us even more suspicious. We should go."

Leo was trying hard to be the most composed of the three, but internally he was in a shambles. His mind was racing a mile a minute, and the strands of each individual thought were becoming more tangled by the second.

Without wasting a moment, the trio hurried out of the small room, down the maze of boxes, and back through the vents. Finally making sure no one saw them, they exited the closet into the empty hallway.

"Ok, ok, so what's our plan?" Although Leo said it out loud, it was more directed at himself than to the others. He turned to look at his companions.

"Why are you guys staring at me? Is there something on my face or something?"

"Why are you asking us what we should do?" Locke said. "If I know you like I think I do, you have already come up with about three or four feasible plans already, haven't you?"

"Well, I have some ideas. But shouldn't we all discuss this before we do something??"

This time it was Lily who cut in with a quiet but an impactful voice. "We both trust you . . . We don't need to waste time discussing the pros and cons of every idea we all have. Leo, you're such a kind person I don't think you ever even notice, but whenever we need to formulate a plan, you always let us speak our minds, but every time, we always just go with your plans anyway. You may not even realize it yourself, but your plans are always the best choice.

"Unlike the two of us, your plans consider each of our strengths and weaknesses so well, sometimes it seems like you can somehow see the future and already know the outcome before we even try."

At her words, Leo turned to Locke, who was nodding his head in agreement. "It's true. I believe whatever plan you've come up with is our best option. So, don't keep us waiting. Spit it out already."

Leo was almost taken aback; he had no idea that either of them thought that way. He was sure that they always helped to contribute to the formulation of their plans in the past. Or was he just being naive?

The more he thought about it, the less he could refute Lily's statement. This whole time they had just been playing along, and he had never even realized. Already in a shaken state, Leo's mind seemed to be coming apart at the very seams. He couldn't help but kick himself at his lack of self-awareness.

How could he have never realized after all this time? They always joked about him being the leader of their group, but now it struck Leo like a ton of bricks. What he had thought of as only a simple joke, to Lily and Locke had been completely genuine.

"Leo are you ok?" Lily waved a hand in front of Leo's frozen face, jarring him back to reality.

"Oh, I'm sorry. I was just trying to remember something."

Snapping back to the situation at hand, Leo looked at the worried expressions of his two beloved comrades. Their expressions of worry and fear cut deep into Leo, as if they were silently begging for him to tell them some grandiose plan that would calm them and give them all a sense of direction in a sea of storms.

At that moment, a sense of artificial clarity washed over Leo's mind. He had to be strong for these two. All he wanted was for them to be happy, and he would do whatever it took to make it so, even if he must fake being confident in the face of his own fear and uncertainty. *I cannot, I will not, let them down due to my own shortcomings.* They trusted him. He would not abuse that gift.

Taking a deep breath, he said, "Ok, listen close you two, I have a plan. We are going to try to meet with the director on the forty-seventh floor. We'll disclose all that we know about the robot and the incident, then possibly tell about our secret hideout. It will be easier for us to come clean now rather than having them find out through their investigation. If all goes well, we'll just be punished, and we won't look like spies or traitors, just some naughty children."

Both Lily and Locke adamantly nodded their heads in agreement, and the trio set off in the direction of the nearest lift.

5

EYES TO SEE, EARS TO HEAR

IT WAS STILL A VERY RISKY PLAN. However, it was a much safer option than the alternative. But actually managing to reach the director in order to come clean would be much easier said than done. The real issue was gaining entry to the forty-seventh floor.

Within the facility, the forty-seventh floor was infamous. It was forbidden to all but a few select staff. It touted the highest level of security possible. No one truly knew what was housed on that floor; however, that did not stop plenty of wild rumors from spreading.

Leo, of course, had heard many of them, from researching super-advanced military weaponry all the way to housing a special spa resort reserved only for the upper echelon of the facility.

Just to get access to the forty-seventh floor one had to ride one of only a few special lifts that stopped there. Even before reaching the floor, they had their IDs and retinas scanned just to be permitted to get off at the floor's military checkpoint.

To Leo's surprise, there were no issues. But as they got off the elevator and approached the intimidating guarded checkpoint, the full weight of what they were doing really sank in.

Abruptly, an unfriendly, disembodied voice rang out through the crackling speaker by the large steel doors flanked by numerous unmanned gun turrets. *"State your business."*

The tension in the air was almost tangible as the intimidating remote turrets sprang to life.

Leo cleared his tight throat, making sure to speak loudly and clearly. "We've come to speak with Director Anderson. We were told to come to speak with him about the disturbance that happened in the dining hall."

There was a brief moment of silence, only filled by the slight static of the intercom system. The three could feel the turrets focusing on them as they tried their best to stand perfectly still.

"The director had to take an emergency call and never arrived here. If you need to see him, he should be in his office on the command level. Now if you have no further business here, you are ordered to leave at once. This is a restricted area."

"Thank you for your help," Leo said.

The trio gave a quick and pristine salute, and they turned and hurried to the elevator. They remained quiet all the way to the floor that contained the command center.

Breaking the oppressive silence, Locke spoke in a semisarcastic manner as they stepped into the hallway. "Well, this is going better than we expected so far. At least now we don't have to watch our backs around those turrets. Geez, those things creep me out."

Leo nodded. "The way that they always follow your movements is very creepy."

Lily folded her arms and puffed out her cheeks. "Hey! don't call them creepy! I helped to design most of those things' internal systems. Model AGN-115 is one of my pride and joys."

"Geez, what is up with your naming system?" Locke said.

"Couldn't you think of something shorter and that actually made sense for once?!"

Locke continued to bicker with Lily as they approached the much smaller set of metal doors that lead to the command center.

"State your business."

Unlike a few minutes before, this time the voice came from a rather lonely looking soldier standing guard in front of the door to the command center.

"We were told that Director Anderson was here. We have just come from the forty-seventh floor, and we have information about the incident in the dining hall that we must report directly to him."

Looking over the three carefully, the guard finally responded. His tone momentarily softened, surprising Leo.

"Long time no see, eh? The guards there just radioed and told me to expect some company."

At the guard's words, Leo looked closer and, after a moment, realized it was the same guard that had helped him earlier. Only this time his helmet was pulled low over his face, trying subtly to hide a rather large bruise covering part of his face.

"Oh, it's you! I was looking for you earlier at the celebration. I wanted to thank you for helping me."

The guard raised his helmet slightly. "Don't mention it, kid. I wasn't there because, as you can see, I had some rather annoying business that I had to take care of. Don't worry about it."

Looking at the guard's face, Leo felt a twinge of guilt.

"Still, thank you." It was a simple phrase, but those words carried a lot of weight in the facility.

"Just get going. You don't wanna keep the director waiting.

I would prefer it if I didn't have to go through anymore 'emergency training' today, if you get my meaning."

The guard covered his face as he returned his helmet, but Leo could tell he was smiling. "Yes sir! But before I forget . . . can I ask for your name?"

Seemingly taken by surprise, the soldier hesitated. "Uh . . . the name's Briggs, Sergeant First Class Kyle Briggs"

Leo etched the name into his memory as the trio respectfully saluted and then entered as the sergeant held one of the doors open.

Approaching the director's office, they checked over each other's appearance quickly, and Leo knocked on the door.

The door opened and they briskly stepped into the spacious office. The sole occupant of the room was on the phone.

"Thank you for this interesting information, Director Lewis. Be sure to thank the director general for me. I'm positive the troops and information he collected will prove to be invaluable in the coming operation."

Director Anderson motioned for the trio to come in and sit on three comfortable-looking chairs in front of his desk. As they sank into their chairs, the director hung up and addressed them in an uncharacteristically animated fashion, causing Leo to feel a bit uneasy.

"So-o-o, a little birdy told me that you three have been looking for me? It also happened to tell me you might have some interesting information for me about the little commotion that happened earlier, hmm?"

He said all this while moving his hands in a dramatic manner like a conductor.

"But before that, I need to ask something important . . . Would you like to graduate from the academy early and start working directly under me, effective immediately?"

Leo could see Lily and Locke were caught as much off guard by the director's abrupt question as he was. All they could do was to stare at him with blank expressions. Although he phrased it as a question, it was all too clear by his demeanor and expression that refusal was not an option.

"Wha-wha—"

"Now, now." The director cut off Leo before he could complete his thought and waved his hand as if to calm the stammering Leo. "I shall tell you all the details of what I'm offering. In simple terms, I would like you to become my personal eyes and ears within the facility. Unlike some of the others under my command, you all have lived your entire lives within these walls.

"I can tell you care greatly for Tessera, and you believe in our vision for the future. As such special individuals, I can see no better alternative than to use you three, possibly one of this facility's strongest assets. For it is not technology or weapons that make humanity strong; it is the human mind that grants us such strength."

This was not what they had been expecting when they made their plan to come clean to the director and beg for leniency. It was such a shock that Leo could feel his companion's eyes darting to him as if they were silently asking him for some sort of direction.

"That . . . that would be an honor, sir. But do you think we are truly ready for such a task? Wouldn't there be other . . . more suitable individuals for such a task???"

"You three are the perfect ones for this particular job, as this pertains to the information you were about to give me, was it not?"

It was obvious he was referring to the incident earlier that day.

"The department heads and I believe that the incident earlier was no accident. It is more than likely we have a corporate spy within our midst."

He straightened his posture, interlaced his fingers, and placed his hands on the table.

"This is highly confidential, but this is not the first incident to happen within this facility within the last few months, although the others were very minor in comparison, just some misplaced maps and such. But factoring in today's events, the pattern is becoming all too clear.

"I would like you three to investigate behind the scenes to the best of your ability and report directly to me. The fewer people who know, the better when it comes to dealing with spies such as these."

"We understand sir; we cannot allow any outsiders to harm our precious Tessera in any way. We will gladly accept your offer."

It was Locke who had quickly and calmly responded to the director's explanation. He must have seen that Leo and Lily were in no state to answer effectively.

The director clapped his hands together. "That's splendid! With you three working behind the scenes, I believe this matter will be solved quickly. Don't let me down. I have such high hopes for you three."

Reaching into his desk he then casually tossed a small black key card onto the desk. "This is a gift for the three of you to use; it is an Alpha-level clearance card. It will allow you all to access most parts of the facility unopposed, just flash that and you should not have any issue in all areas excluding Omega-level locations. Just don't let this new power go to your heads, and you should be just fine."

A rather large, mischievous grin formed on his face. "Oh, and before I forget, what was the information you wonderful children came all this way to tell me? It must have been rather important, hmm?"

The director had finally asked the question that Leo had been dreading for the duration of their conversation. The director's question was a more effective sucker punch than the colonel's actual sucker punch. Ever since the director brought up his proposal, Leo's brain had been in overdrive trying to come up with counterstrategy after counterstrategy. In the end, Leo just prayed telling half of the truth would be enough.

"Oh . . . To be honest sir, you mostly covered what we wanted to tell you . . . But," Leo waved vaguely towards Lily, who was sitting next to him, "Lily here was the one who designed and built the robot that was involved in the incident earlier. After the fact, she went back and went through all the blueprints and she concluded that someone must have disabled one of the safety mechanisms, which could have led directly to it going out of control. So, we were coming here to tell you that it was most likely sabotaged by someone who knew how the system operated."

The director listened closely and nodded. "It's good that we are all on the same page. With your testimony, it adds even more validity to the theory of a spy in our midst. I thank you for your report, and I wish for you to get to work immediately."

Reaching back into his desk, he pulled out an officially stamped envelope and tossed it on top of the key card.

"Unfortunately, even given my position, we still need to follow proper protocol and procedure." Sighing in deep irritation and kneading his temples, the director said, "In order for you to be moved under my direct command, I need to give these orders of separation to your head instructor to force through your graduation. If you would be so kind, could you deliver this to Ms. Meli? It should be processed quickly, and then you can begin your investigation tomorrow."

The three stood up simultaneously, and Lily reached over to accept the envelope and the Alpha-level key card. "We will deliver it to her with all due haste. Thank you again, sir. It is an honor for you to have so much faith in us."

The director waved off Lily's praise. "No, no, no. Thank you all for being such special children. Consider this an early graduation present." He reached into his desk yet again and retrieved two small, plain boxes.

"Be sure to not open them until after tomorrow. One is a gift from me, and the other is from the colonel." He gave a subtle wink as Locke accepted the boxes, and Leo gave a graceful salute, which the director cheerfully returned.

In the hallway outside the command center, the trio breathed a heavy sigh of relief.

"Thank God that somehow worked out," Leo said. "I can't believe our luck."

Locke frowned. "I don't know; something still doesn't sit right with me. That all seemed too perfect. I understand why he wanted us to become spies for him. For the most part, people would overlook us, and we have a decent reputation, but I still don't get it . . . If they've known about other incidents, then why call us in now?"

"Maybe it's gotten just that out of their control?" Lily said. "But remember what we overheard. Something definitely isn't right. They talked about us, but I didn't understand it at all."

They talked over all the events that had just transpired as they made their way to the residential quarters of their academic supervisor, Ms. Meli.

• • •

As they walked through the area which housed most of the members of academia, many bystanders shouted words of praise as they passed.

"Good job!"

"I always knew you guys were special."

"With you, Tessera is going to be unstoppable."

Since being paraded out on stage, it seemed they had become quite the hot topic within the facility. Growing tired of acknowledging each and every comment, they finally reached the door marked with the name Melissa M. Meli. Leo reached up to knock on the door, however, his knuckles only managed to hit thin air. The door, which had seemingly sensed their presence, had opened of its own accord. Taken a little by surprise, Locke called into the open doorway.

"Hello? Ms. Meli, we came to deliver an envelope to you from the director . . . Anyone home?"

There was no response to his call.

Lily was the first to sheepishly speak up to break the awkward silence. "Should we go in and put it on her desk? It is urgent after all. Plus, I don't think she will get mad, since it's an order from the director, right?"

Thinking about it for a few moments, Locke couldn't disagree with her sound reasoning. He and Leo nodded as they stepped inside the dimly lit room.

"Do either of you see her office?" Leo said. "It's so dark in here I can barely see anything."

Although she lived alone, being of relatively high rank and status, Ms. Meli had a rather spacious living arrangement. There were many rooms, as opposed to the simple bedrooms that they themselves occupied. They decided that the fastest way would be to split up. They each took a section of the apartment to search for the door to her office. "Try your best to not disturb anything," Leo said. "I don't want to weather the wrath of Ms. Meli one last time for something as simple as knocking over and breaking something important."

Locke managed to find the open door to her study. He carefully entered while quietly calling out to his companions.

The room was an utter disaster. There were files, loose pages, and discarded food containers scattered across every inch of the floor, desk, and chairs within the cramped room.

Finally finding the light switch, something immediately drew Locke's gaze. He traversed the organized chaos, making his way over to the cluttered desk. Something was sticking out from among a mass of papers. It appeared to be a map or an architectural layout of some kind, but what shocked Locke the most was what was stamped in big, bold, red letters across the top:

FLOOR 47
[Top Secret: Eyes Only]

Before Locke had time to fully digest the sight before him, he heard the sounds of his companions approaching the doorway. When he looked up, however, he was surprised to see the owner of the room standing in the shadow of the doorway behind Leo and Lily. Something in her right hand glistened faintly as she flicked her hand, pointing into the room.

Did she catch them snooping? Many questions raced through his mind as Leo and Lily walked, dead silently and rather stiffly, over the threshold of the office doorway. As his brain tried its best to come up with a good excuse for snooping around in her office, Locke was sure that Ms. Meli was going to yell at him for catching him in there. He prepared himself to be endlessly reprimanded for his inexcusable behavior, but shockingly the high-pitched voice never came.

Her demeanor within the shadows seemed almost ghoul-like, almost as though it was someone else wearing the clothes of Ms. Meli.

It was at that moment that the rest of the lights in the hall and office suddenly turned on, illuminating the terrified faces of his companions as well as a long metallic object pointed menacingly towards their backs.

"So, were you sent here to spy on me?" Ms. Meli said. "You must have been watching me closely. I left this room for only a moment, and yet here you three are . . ."

Her voice was unlike Locke had ever heard it before, it was as cold as ice and lacked all semblance of her usually sing-song tone.

"To make a mistake after all this time . . . It should really be me who deserves to be shot . . ."

She seemed to be speaking to herself. Locke had a terrible feeling well up in the pit of his stomach as a thought popped into his mind. Ms. Meli must be the spy that they were tasked to look for.

As he tried to steady his own shaking hands, Locke internally laughed at this strange turn of events. He would have never imagined that they would have found their target so soon, but he had also assumed that they would have lived long enough to tell the tale.

"I'm sorry, Leo, Lily, Locke, but it seems I must close the book on your short lives. I am truly sorry it must come to this, but I must not be discovered . . . not yet."

Her stiff expression showed her seriousness, but her eyes shone with what could only be described as a slight disappointment.

As she leveled the gun at Lily's frozen body, Locke's body reacted on its own out of sheer animalistic desperation. Without thinking, he began to speak with the confidence of a veteran soldier all to familiar with the fear of death.

"We can get you inside of the forty-seventh floor. We know a secret way. There's something you need in there, right?"

Ms. Meli slightly lowered her gun and looked directly at Locke. "Just because you saw the map does not mean you hold any incentive for me keeping you three alive. I'm sure you would say anything in this situation if it meant I spared you."

What she said was true. Without proof or any assurance, she would never trust them.

"I have proof! Just let me show you." Locke slowly pointed at the map, trying his best to not make any sudden moves. He could see the looks of disbelief on Leo's and Lily's faces out of the corner of his eye. "Please let me show you . . . You have nothing to lose. I am telling the truth."

His inner confidence finally matched his external bravado, and he took a step towards the desk. Ms. Meli stood firm as she watched him walk over to the map.

"You have thirty seconds, and if you try to lie . . . then you'll be the last one to die."

Locke had never felt such tension. Leo looked like he wanted to break down in tears on the spot. Locke could tell Lily felt utterly powerless by the way her shaking hands had become tight fists.

"Look here." Locke pointed down at the blueprint on the desk. "I knew it . . . These looked familiar, I just couldn't remember how."

Half talking to himself, half to his companions, Locke looked up. "There is a surefire way to break into the floor without being spotted by using these." He used his index finger to trace a path on the map as Ms. Meli took a step closer. "I recognized this ventilation system because it is directly connected to our secret base. It starts here . . . and comes out right at this junction right over here."

At his explanation, both Leo and Lily turned to each other in amazement. "He's right," Leo said. "That's our base right there. I can't believe you caught that."

Ms. Meli flicked her gun at them. "*Silence you two!* Let me think . . ."

Locke said, "Just because you now know how to get in, doesn't mean you'll be able to use it. The path is very small and dangerous. Although, we could go for you . . ."

Locke's delivery was perfect, and the tables were slowly turning.

"If I let you go, what would stop you from reporting me the

minute I let you out of this room? And if you were to get caught and interrogated, I would be stuck in the same situation but with more loose ends."

Leo finally found his voice. "You could hold one of us as collateral as the others go. Then we wouldn't rat you out even if we were caught."

Ms. Meli stroked her chin while pondering the idea, the whole time never relaxing her grip on the gun.

"Hmm . . . that does seem like a good idea. After you do break in, you'll appear to have been the spies or, at least, accomplices. Breaking into such a restricted area, our fates would be linked . . . Hmm, I do like the thought of there being four of us, rather than just me trying to hide my tracks."

Her judgment was sound. It would be a beneficial offer for her to take, indeed, but not so much for the three standing nervously waiting for her final decision.

"I—I accept your offer, and because you graciously suggested it, I'll take you, Leo, as my hostage. You were always the most troublesome after all. It would be in my best interest to keep my eye on you."

Ms. Meli's face broke into a malicious smile, one that Locke had never seen her make before and it shook him to the bone. She asked, "How long will it take you to break in and then return here?"

Quickly doing some mental calculations, Locke said, "If we can take the map with us, possibly two to three hours."

"I don't want you to take your sweet time and come up with any foolish plans now . . . So I'll give you not a second longer than sixty minutes from the moment you step outside this room."

This new Ms. Meli or, rather, the real Ms. Meli was terrifying and much sharper than her old persona would have let on. She instantly undercut Locke's estimated time, for she had guessed that he had well overestimated the time they would need. Forcing them to be in a rush severely hindered their attempt to come up with any sort of counterstrategy.

"Fine," Leo said. "It's a deal then. Now tell us what it is you want us to do."

With the same frozen smile, Ms. Meli began to describe to them in detail what they needed to do in order to escape with their lives.

6

LINES ON A MAP

"LEO'S TIMER STARTS NOW."

As Ms. Meli's door slammed shut behind them, the only sounds that could be heard in the hallway were the loud footfalls of Lily and Locke as they sprinted down the hall.

The task they had been assigned seemed almost impossible for the sixty minutes they were given, but fear drove them on, nonetheless. Even as their feet began to drag from exhaustion, they finally turned the last corner before the storage closet door.

Normally around this hour in the evening, the facility's staff would be getting off their shifts and returning to their quarters, but due to the day's events, the halls were eerily desolate. Lily and Locke had made great time reaching their first destination.

Quickly entering the storage closet, Lily began to open the entrance to the vent. At the same time, Locke was going over the vast assignment they had been given only a tiny window of time to complete and breaking it down into steps.

Step One: Return to base (completed).
Step Two: Read the map and gather supplies to climb several
floors worth of ventilation system.

Step Three: Find the subventilation system maintenance hatch for the forty-seventh floor.

Step Four: Disable or sneak around the mountains of security drones, doors, soldiers, and turrets, and enter without being seen or captured.

Step Five: Find the long-range encrypted transmitter, and send out the message he had received from Ms. Meli to who knows who.

Upon reaching this step in his mind, Locke gave an exasperated sigh. How the hell was he even going to find and use all this equipment??? He had never even used a transmitter in his entire life, and now the fate of his friend's life was at stake.

He did not even know if they could traverse the forty-seventh floor within the time limit. At least for the vent shafts they had a map to use, although even that did not go into any detail about most of the locations on the floor itself.

Step Six: Plant the false evidence that they were given.

Step Seven: Sabotage the transmitter.

Step Eight: Escape and meet up with Leo and Ms. Meli at the rendezvous point.

Going through these eight steps repeatedly, it seemed impossible given any time limit, let alone sixty minutes, but they still had to try.

Crawling through the vents for what seemed like the millionth time that day, Locke could only envision what Leo must be enduring at the hands of Ms. Meli. He shuddered at the mere thought. It was Lily's voice behind him, however, that suddenly brought everything back into perspective.

"Don't worry about Leo; he will be just fine. Has he ever failed us before? This time it is up to us. We must not squander the faith he puts in us. We will succeed, and everything will be ok, you'll see."

She spoke with the resolve and confidence of having already seen the future.

Unlike Locke, who would have said those words but would never have truly believed them, he knew Lily's confident words only mirrored how she truly felt. Locke greatly admired her confidence in their abilities and their close bond of friendship. Her strong will and confidence helped to give his own weaker conviction the boost it needed to push forward.

• • •

Leo sat with his back towards the door, and Ms. Meli had her gun trained on him while watching the door behind him like a hawk. He knew that, if anyone were to enter, both he and the interloper would be killed instantly, He only prayed that no one would come make a house call.

The effects of adrenalin were finally starting to wear off, and the uncomfortable silence between the two of them had reached a deafening roar.

Leo's perception of time was starting to deteriorate as they sat silently staring at each other for what seemed like an extremely long time. As he continued to stare at the blank face of the woman he thought he had known, he began to notice the effects of complacency slowly creep over her hardened expression.

Feeling it to be a better time than any, he began to open his mouth to speak, but Ms. Meli broke the silence first. "It must be jarring to see me like this . . . Thinking you know someone, then to have your expectation turned on its head is an experience I am all too familiar with."

She gave a great sigh as her face slightly relaxed. However, the gun in her hand was telling a different story entirely.

"In my line of work, I sometimes forget where the part I play ends and where my true self begins. It has been so long since I have shed this mask. It feels rather strange but, at the same time, rather refreshing."

Ms. Meli was almost speaking to herself rather than to Leo, but he chose to remain silent and closely listen for any detail she might let slip that would give him any sort of advantage. Besides the gun, she wielded the most versatile and powerful weapon of all, information. She knew all there was to know about him and the others, but now all the precious information he thought he knew about her was all but worthless.

"Since now we are accomplices, there should be little harm in telling you a little about myself, to kill some time."

Leo tried not to look surprised. That was the last thing he would have expected a spy to say to him. In her profession, information was worth more than human life, and now she was going to willingly tell him possibly damaging information. It must be a trap, a lie.

Her gaze seemed to understand the thoughts going through Leo's mind.

"You're very perceptive. Everything I might tell you could be nothing more than an elaborate lie," she said, as if he had spoken his thoughts aloud. "But consider . . . It may possibly be the truth. That is for you and only you to decide. You may not understand it now, but there is a reason I am going to tell you this information. It may prove invaluable to all of our survival in the near future."

Ms. Meli looked off into the corner of the room as she finished, her cryptic words only proved to confuse Leo even more.

Leo glared at her. "Fine. Tell me your silly story. It's not like we have anything better to do while we wait for Lily and Locke to do your dirty work."

A sinister smile spread across her face. "Ha . . . I knew I picked correctly. You are definitely an interesting one." Though she appeared to be relaxed as she finally began to spin her tale, the barrel of the gun never moved off Leo for even a moment.

• • •

Having finally dropped down into the familiar mountain of boxes piled high to the ceiling, Lily and Locke were happily greeted by Rusty. As he approached them, however, he seemed to notice the absence of his favorite human jumping bag and turned his mechanical head in an inquisitive manner.

Lily spoke softly to her mechanical canine as she rubbed the cold ears being nuzzled against her hand. "It's ok, boy. Leo has his hands tied right now, and we need to hurry to get them free. We're going to need your help."

As if understanding the situation by her tone alone, Rusty looked up and gave a silent but vigorous nod of compliance. His tail was swishing so fast he looked as though he was about to take off and fly away.

Spreading out the map on Lily's workbench, Locke looked for the fastest and, relatively speaking, the safest path.

At the same time Locke was pouring every ounce of his brain power into finding a route, given their strict timetable, Lily and Rusty were running around, finding anything they could need.

"I need a backpack, lantern, tool kit . . . oh and some rope!"

Lily gave orders to Rusty as they toppled mountains of boxes to find what they needed. Every time she found an item, she gave it to Rusty, who was acting as quick transportation between Lily and Locke.

Rusty approached Locke for the fifth time within minutes. Only glancing down for a moment, Locke reflexively reached down and patted Rusty's cold metallic head, who whimpered in approval, as he took the item. This time, Rusty had been holding a small crossbow-looking contraption within his mechanical jaws.

"*Lily! We are not going to kill anyone!*"

"Are you sure?"

He hoped she was joking to lighten the mood. Not once had he ever considered taking the life of another person before. He'd never had the need to. But Lily had made Locke consider the possibility that he might indeed be forced to kill, either for his own life or, worse, the lives of his two closest friends.

Locke began to carefully draw out the path he had chosen onto a separate sheet of loose paper. It would be better if they each carried something just in case they had to split up.

"All right, Rusty, I think I've found the best path. Go get Lily for me."

Just as he finished, Lily looked over his shoulder. She had a large backpack hanging from her shoulders. It looked as though both her and Rusty could fit comfortably within it. Locke could only shake his head at the sight of the small girl and her dog looking as if they were going to climb the world's tallest mountain.

"Do you plan on bringing the whole room with us?" he said, pointing to the map. "You know we have to climb this elevator shaft, right?"

"I only packed the essentials. My tool kit, rope, water, snacks, some clothes, harnesses for us and Rusty, flashlights, and just a little composition C-4."

"Whoa, whoa, whoa! What did you just say?"

"My tool kit, rope, water, food, some clothes, harnesses for us and—"

"No no no. What was the last one? Say that one again."

"Oh, you mean the C-4?"

Locke could not believe what he had just heard, never mind mind how she had even gotten it. This girl standing meekly in front of him was carrying a high explosive in her overstuffed pack.

"Take that out right now!" Locke said, taking several cautious steps back." The last thing I want is you trying to sneak onto the forty-seventh floor carrying C-4 on your back. Explosives and the element of surprise do not work together!"

Locke couldn't help but to exasperatedly wave his arms as he took several cautious steps away from his utterly insane companion.

Lily wore a confused expression. "It's not for when we break in, silly! It's to destroy the transmitter and create a diversion so we can escape. We will alert them when we start using the transmitter. Also, Ms. Meli told us to sabotage it anyway."

Made momentarily speechless by her sound reasoning, Locke gave a large sigh.

"Uh, fine . . . but no to taking Rusty with us."

Kicking her foot in disappointment, Lily said, "I thought you wouldn't notice I said that . . . Fine, I guess, but I'm gonna take some of my RATS instead."

"Agreed." Locke picked up the maps and stowed one in his own pack.

Reaching down to comfort the robotic dog sitting by her feet, Lily patted Rusty's head as if to say, "good boy" while, at the same time, calling out into the dark.

At her call, an entire army of tiny rodent-like robots materialized from the room's shadowy corners and scurried over to her. She then selected three out of the massive horde of squeaking creatures and placed them in her pack.

"Their sharp teeth will be perfect for cutting wires," Lily said. "And these three have Remote Vision, which will transmit everything they see back to my master controller."

These precise and tiny robots were among Lily's most prized inventions, and her choice to take some of her favorite creations, as well as her willingness to take Rusty along, showed Locke how dedicated she was to getting Leo back safe and sound.

After checking both their packs and the map one last time, they made their way into Lily's secret hideaway and located the small grate on the wall that, when opened, would begin their long and treacherous climb to the forty-seventh floor.

Managing to pull the grate free, they could hear the rush of high-speed machinery mixed with the soft whimper of their canine companion as they peered into the dark abyss.

• • •

"I was born in the vast wastelands of the west, within a small community of devout evangelists," Miss Meli said. "My parents were part of a humanitarian coalition that went from place to place providing medical care and teaching basic medicine to the refugees scattered across the Western Wasteland.

"Shortly before I was born, the local religious leader of the area had heard about the amazing skills of my parents and sent his men to capture them. His plan was to use their famous skills to raise his own popularity and fame among those in the Wasteland and gain more followers.

"To prevent the massacre of the poor village where they were stationed at the time, my parents were willingly taken captive and brought to the man known simply as 'the Apostle.'

"They were held within his settlement for many years and forced to act as the community's only pair of trained doctors. However, after my birth and the inevitable passage of time, my parents transitioned from simply being captives to becoming very respected members of the community, even against the Apostle's will.

"After treating and caring for its members for so long it was only natural that they were eventually seen as saviors instead of slaves. They could have easily escaped by that point, but they did not wish to push hard travels on one as young as myself at that time, so out of the sheer kindness of their hearts they chose to remain.

"Everything was going well until I turned the age of ten. Then the howling winds of change began to blow again. The Apostle, who had been the sole leader of the entire region for quite some time, suddenly died. His absence caused a vacuum, and subsequently a power struggle began.

"Power is a tempting thing after all, and many will do anything to get it. My father, being at this time a very respected member of the community, was quickly approached and was asked to become their next leader. The common people deemed his medical feats borderline holy miracles.

"My father, being a kind man, seeing all the good he could do as the new leader, gladly accepted.

"That did not last long, however. As you can imagine, many hardliners did not take too well to the idea of an outsider becoming the next Apostle of God, and so a plot was hatched. The Apostle's hardliner faction managed to plant false evidence implicating my father as the one who caused the death of the original Apostle to usurp his position. That was all it took to trigger the masses; in the end, our only option was to leave everything and run for our very lives.

"However, during our frantic escape, my poor mother was caught. My father had to struggle to hold me back as I desperately fought to go after her.

"I always think back to that moment . . . If only I could have been stronger. Why did that have to happen to us. My parents were so kind . . . Why is this world so cruel? A deep burning hatred was born within me on that day.

"As my father and I escaped over the nearby mountain range, we could smell the distant smoke from the fire. In Amari, the village I was raised in . . . Do you know what they do to those who have defied God?"

Her eyes glazed over, and she stared off into the distance, seemingly to a place far removed from their current location.

Inhaling deeply, the pain in her voice was almost palpable. "They would crucify them . . . then burn them alive for all to see. They said it was in order to purify their souls before God."

Her tone then suddenly trembled, and her glazed eyes focused and became those of pure hatred, seething with rage.

"After all my parents did for them . . . Those animals . . . They deserve . . ." Taking another deep breath, she regained her composure. Leo, who had been enthralled by her tale, began to sympathize with her story. He hoped he wasn't playing right into her hands.

• • •

Hanging twenty feet above the small hole where they had entered the abyss, Lily and Locke were trying their best to not be run over.

-*Whoosh*-

Yet another elevator car passed mere inches from their backs. Ignoring it, Lily continued to steadily climb up the rope in the cramped elevator shaft.

Below her, about a body's length between them, Locke had a rather unique expression frozen on his face as he watched the elevator car race past them at a lethal speed.

Within this shaft, there seemed to be a passing elevator car every sixty seconds or so. They were climbing from vent to vent within the shaft in an extremely tiny area between the rails that guided the elevator cars and the concrete walls that enclosed the shaft.

So far, they had managed to progress by hooking ropes onto the horizontal vanes of the ventilation grates. Sadly, they could only progress so fast because at every new floor the vent locations mysteriously switched sides in the shaft.

Whenever they reached a new floor, they tossed the rope and crossed over the deadly pathway of the high-speed elevator car to the safety of the other side, right after each car went flying past them.

So far, twenty feet had taken them about five minutes, and they still had over eighty feet to go before reaching the forty-seventh floor.

After the last car was out of sight, Locke relaxed his death grip on his sole lifeline and reached up and continued to climb.

"This was a terrible idea! Who the hell came up with this plan again!?!" he yelled up to Lily, who was making quick work of the climb.

Her focus was the placement of her hands, where to reach next, would the next spot hold their weight. She skillfully disregarded anything else around her, and her current focus seemed unbreakable, since she easily ignored the dangerous proximity of the cars, as well as Locke's feeble attempt at complaining.

Locke was showing his fear, but Lily's expression was as unchanging as stone.

"Hey! Are you listening to me?" Locke said. "Hey! Stop climbing, already! We need to take this vent over here!" His frantic, high-pitched yelling finally snapped Lily out of her singular focus.

He had stopped and was trying his best to get her attention, yelling and waving his free hand, while at the same time holding on for dear life with his other. They had reached the floor where they needed to take a bit of a detour through the vent system, in order to reach another adjacent elevator shaft. The one they were currently in did not have access to the forty-seventh floor.

As Locke waited for Lily to climb back down to him, he pulled the map out of his bag and skimmed over it again. There was nothing worse than to waste time.

Following the outlined path he had made, Locke couldn't help criticize the architects who designed these shafts. "They really made it a pain to navigate. How does anyone even manage to get around and fix these things?"

"So, this is the one?" Lily asked as she pulled herself alongside Locke at the louvered grating of the horizontal ventilation shaft.

"Yeah, this is the one. From here we need to crawl through until we reach the adjacent shaft, then climb up a few more floors. But from this map, it seems something is in the next shaft beside the standard tracks like this one. See, look."

Locke pointed towards their current position and then, with his finger, moved along to where a strange marking was shown within the next shaft. It appeared to be indicating something of relative importance, but when Locke tried to look up the symbol in the index it was not there. It most likely was on another page of the map that they did not have.

"Well, I guess we'll see when we get there, won't we?" Lily said.

Locke carefully folded up the map and placed it back in his bag. He pointed to the vent. "After you. What do they always say? Ladies first?"

"Why do I always have to go first? You're the one who has the map and already knows the way. Is this all it takes to get you scared, hmm?"

"N-no. It's just you need to open the vent. And . . . and you're a faster climber than me anyways."

"Oh . . . Well, if that's the case then I guess I have to. But when we get out of here, I'm going to take you out for more exercise once in a while."

Finally finished with their usual playful banter, Lily reached into her bag and pulled out her tool kit. From within her extensive kit, she withdrew a small blow torch, gloves, and a pristine set of goggles. She bluntly pushed Locke aside and got straight to work cutting the vent from its enclosure. Watching helplessly from the sidelines, Locke knew not to interrupt her. Whenever she put on her equipment and got to work in earnest, God himself knew not to get in her way.

Lily made quick work of the once sturdy vent, returning her gear to her bag. She shrugged at Locke in a mocking manner and made her way first into the dark and musty duct.

• • •

"So, after our escape, my father and I made our way over desolate mountain range after desolate mountain range. We did this for what seemed like weeks. Even though we had not come across a living soul for the entirety of our journey, we constantly felt like we were being hunted. Not by the mountain animals, which we occasionally encountered, but by the true kings of the Wasteland, humans.

"But one night my father and I were being stalked by a pack of wolves. We were hopelessly outnumbered. I honestly thought it was the end for us. As we sensed the pack tightening around us like a noose, the only weapon we could muster was a small fire.

"As my father stood in front of me, wielding his pathetic torch, all I could do was pray. I hated myself. Even after what happened to my mother, I still didn't have the strength to do anything. It was at that moment that I just gave up. I accepted that I was pathetic. I even wished for the release of death. At least then I could be together with both my mother and father, after our inevitable fate at the teeth of the wolves.

"It seems to be a running trend in my life, but what I wished for did not come to pass. Just as one of the wolves lunged at my father, multiple thunderous sounds pierced the air all around us. The pack of wolves all fell at once. For a moment I thought that my prayers had finally been answered.

"In reality, a small group of well-armed men appeared. They gave us some food and water and told us that they had been out surveying the area and happened to find our tracks along with those of the wolf pack that had been stalking us.

"The three men before us seemed, from initial impressions, kind and skilled individuals. They each carried a rifle and wore a military-style uniform with a strange symbol I had never seen before on their sleeves. As they spoke with us, they told us all about the area in which they were based and about the organization that they worked for. They offered to take us to their outpost, which they said was not too far away. They said that it welcomed refugees such as us, who would be willing to work for food and shelter.

"I couldn't believe our luck. We were saved.

"So many things happened so fast. It felt very much like a dream. We followed the soldiers back to their base, which seemed more like a small, fortified town rather than a proper military base. They gave us some food and a place to sleep, and the next day we were sent to work. Like with most dreams, however, it didn't last very long.

"It did not take very long for my seemingly wonderful dream to turn into yet another nightmare. In hindsight, where we were brought was nothing more than a slave work camp for that organization.

"We were tricked into entering the lion's den, with no power or means of escape. Once we had entered, we were forced to give up everything we had with us, made to put on shabby clothes with that same strange symbol on them, and forced to work under the threat of starvation.

"The work was grueling. My father was put to work in the mines of one of the many mountains that surrounded the camp. I was forced to toil mending the soldiers' clothing, among other more unsavory things. We were far from the only ones who were forced to work. It seemed our new masters had also tricked many others from nearby towns with their sweet words.

"They were always watching us, making sure that no one could escape or slack in their work. As time went on, it was not uncommon for one of my coworkers to never again show up in his or her spot beside me.

"Years like this went by. I saw many faces come and go . . . many of whom were dear friends. It is a strange thing for one who has never been a slave to be forced to work under such conditions. Unlike my time in Amari, being a slave was almost a freeing experience. I know that seems contradictory. Even though my body was pushed to the breaking point, one's perception can become distorted.

"But although my body was forced to work, within my own mind I was completely free.

"Being a slave gave me a new perspective. It helped me learn to cherish and enjoy the smallest things in life, the love of a father, the blandest scrap of bread, the morning sunrise, all of which I had never given a second thought before. I had found a small amount of peace within all that suffering.

"Looking back, Tessera did a magnificent job of conditioning all of its slaves. To actually find peace while being a slave, I can't help but laugh at it now. What a load of crap.

"The small semblance of inner peace I had, however, was smashed the moment my father became extremely sick due to his grueling work in the mines. His last few months were awful. I tried to help him as much as I could, even pleading with our captors to help save him, but they merely scoffed at the idea. To them no slave was that valuable. So, I was forced to watch my father slowly die, the man who I looked up to and loved like no other, the last of my family . . .

"Forced to see his killers day after day as they beat, starved, and killed so many others, my short-lived inner peace became a distant memory. All that kept me going was the new raging fire within my heart.

"Luckily, the revenge I longed for came much sooner than I had hoped. Only a few weeks after my father's death, my saviors, my new family, came for me, bringing death to all my enemies. The camp where we were held was attacked by my current employer and new family, Penrose Industries.

"The sounds of the battle were tremendous, and there were many losses on both sides. As we slaves huddled together, believing we were sure to die, Penrose soldiers captured the compound. All those who remained were then driven like cattle to the center of the camp and presented as prizes to the victors.

"The Penrose commander addressed us while standing in front of the remaining captured Tessera officers. He congratulated us on being rescued by the kindness of Penrose's heart and explained in detail about Tessera's terrible transgressions around the globe. He even sent out a call for those who wished to join them in their just fight to stop Tessera's vile plan for world conquest.

"This was the perfect opportunity for me. My soul still burned to take my revenge, not just against that camp but also against the entirety of the organization that made my father's and my suffering possible.

"I was the first and only one to stand. Head held high and eyes burning with desire, I approached the Penrose commander. He seemed shocked that a young girl was the first to come forward, especially one in such a sad state. I could tell from his expression he did not think much of me. Who would, for I was but a small, weak girl.

"The sympathetic look he gave me was full of compassion as he told me that they were not like Tessera and would not force children to fight. All I could do was stare at him. I needed this . . . I needed to do this. I needed to show him, show all of them, that I was not pathetic and worthless.

"My hands reacted without my thinking about it. The next thing I was aware of was the cold steel in my hand and the high-pitched ringing in my ears. I was tackled to the ground before I even realized what I had done.

"I had taken the commander's sidearm and shot one of the Tessera commanders. It was the simple act of pulling that trigger that led me to this current predicament, with you sitting here across from me. After concluding that I was no threat, I was released, and the Penrose commander looked at me with an expression mixed with shock and admiration."

• • •

Locke sneezed.

Crawling through the cramped and musty ventilation system was far more complex than the simple diagram on the map would indicate. The map could never accurately represent the terrible conditions that Lily and Locke were now crawling through. Locke looked ahead as he rubbed his nose. The sheer amount of dust and spider webs was enough to make anyone feel wheezy.

As they approached a four-way junction, Lily stopped and looked down each path. To her surprise, small arrows and symbols could be seen by the faint light from their flashlights as she pointed down each path. "Why of all places would they put markers in here? Do they just assume people are always crawling around the vents? Or maybe they were orientation markers used for workers when this system was being constructed."

That was a possibility, Locke thought as Lily moved closer, and he shined his light upon the map.

"Ok," he said, "judging by these symbols we need to follow this path, and it will directly lead to the shaft that exits right before the forty-seventh floor."

Holding the map up to the different symbols on the walls, they each looked as if they were some kind of warning symbol. Locked looked at the matching symbol of the direction they needed to go, a triangle with a smaller symbol inside of it. The inner symbol looked like a large plus sign. With no other revealing information on the map or on the vent wall, he could only speculate what the meaning was.

Putting the map away, they continued forward until they reached the sudden end of the horizontal shaft. It connected directly into another large vertical shaft, blocking their way forward. Unlike the last one, this one had no ventilation grates to which they could hook their ropes.

Lily looked around. "Well, this is going to be fun. It looks like our only option is to free climb up using the rivets on the walls . . ."

In total shock, and with fear in his voice, Locke stammered.

"Y-you can't be serious. You're telling me we have to climb up without a rope, by hand? We will never be able to make it all the way to the next floor like that!"

"Yeah, it's the only way," Lily said. "I didn't have enough room in my bag to bring my GRAPNEL MARK II. I honestly kind of regret that now." Straining her neck to look up the dark shaft, she sighed a long sigh.

"The best thing I have right now are my MAGG-91s, and I only have one pair. So, I guess we'll have to tie ourselves together, and I'll have to somehow manage to pull you up whenever I reach a large enough ledge."

It was better than doing it barehanded, but Locke could not get out of his head the mental image of himself helplessly dangling from a small rope attached to Lily as she climbed the steel walls using only a pair of homemade magnetic gloves.

"It's not like I don't trust you . . . but will those things actually hold both of us?" Locke looked on as she carefully put on the surprisingly small gloves.

Giving him a big toothy grin, Lily nodded her head. "Don't

worry. I made these things about four times stronger than they needed to be." As she made her way out of the safety of the vent, Locke hoped it would be enough.

Hanging unceremoniously from the rope that connected the two, all Locke could do was to pray that both the rope and Lily's grip would continue to hold. This new shaft was very windy and blew Locke every which way. He waved his arms frantically, trying to swim through the air to the safety of the shaft wall behind him.

"I swear," he yelled out to Lily, who was slowly pulling him up to the next floor, "if I ever have to go crawling through these vents or climbing up these shafts again . . . it will be too soon!"

"Quit complaining! You're heavier than you look, you know! Plus, you're moving around too much. When we get back, I'm gonna put you on a diet, on top of those swimming lessons, heh-heh."

Even while struggling to pull him up, Lily still had the energy to throw verbal jabs.

Just as Locke was a mere arm's reach away from Lily's position, a fierce gust of wind reached them from below. It was so sudden and strong it forced Lily to let go of the rope Locke was hanging from to stabilize herself while she precariously balanced on a small ledge.

Locke screamed at suddenly being dropped. Even though they were connected by the rope, the feeling of dropping even a few feet in this environment was terrifying. He could feel his heart trying to escape his chest as he hung only a few feet below Lily. All his rational thought had vanished, and the only thing repeating itself in his mind was the single phrase:

I do not want to die! I do not want to die!

That same phrase kept repeating in Locke's mind as a snickering Lily finally began to haul him back up the side of the shaft.

"Don't you laugh at me! That was not funny. I literally thought I was about to die!"

Lily let out a small laugh. "I'm only laughing because I don't think I've ever heard you scream like that before. It was kind of adorable, in a weird way."

"Don't you mean in a fear-for-my-life type of way? I've never screamed like that before, because as you know . . . I have never almost fallen to my death in a shaft before!"

It seemed as if Locke's pounding heart could be heard echoing off the metal walls along with Lily's faint snickering as they finished squabbling and continued their journey. Finally exiting the emptiness of the shaft, they started to crawl through the last vent, which Locke prayed would actually exit onto the forty-seventh floor.

• • •

"So, as it turned out, the Penrose commander that I impressed with my little stunt was a very influential member of the Penrose high council. He saw something in me, and after I returned with them to their headquarters, he offered me a shocking proposal.

"He wished for me to go through special military training to become a warrior even though I was still only a young girl. He saw the fire of determination in my eyes, the resolve to become strong, the *need* to become strong for the sake of my goals. I did not hesitate. Never again would I hesitate.

"Though I'll have to admit it, the training was very different than I imagined. I never realized that learning to kill would be so structured and disciplined when done correctly. In a way, becoming a good warrior is not all too different from becoming a master artisan. Unknown to me at the time, I was what one would call an 'artistic genius.'

"Even though I was but a child, I showed a knack for all things related to killing. Knives, guns, poisons, even my bare hands, I was skilled with all of them. I progressed at an incredible rate compared to my more adult comrades, and I quickly became very popular.

"Within just a few months, I was tasked with leading entire teams into the wastelands to hunt for Tessera and their allies. The only problem was even though I was a genius at killing, that did not necessarily translate well into leading others. Sadly, it is very hard to describe your tactics and plans to those who aren't also a genius . . . I found that out the hard way.

"So, after only a few missions in command, I was relieved of standard military duty as they tried to figure out what to do with me, a lone killing machine with the appearance of a young girl. It did not take them long to find the perfect job, one I had never considered.

"What the higher-ups offered to me was training in order to become an assassin. On paper, it was a perfect fit. I got to kill all those who stood against me, and instead of only killing soldiers, I had the possibility of striking much more significant blows to our enemies.

"As the years went on and my kill count became so high that I didn't bother to keep track any longer, I finally realized something. No matter how many soldiers or VIPs I killed, in the end, nothing really seemed to change. Someone would always take their place, and eventually it was as if all my work had never even happened. I grew frustrated. My sole goal was to burn Tessera to the ground, and all the rage within me was focused on that singular task, and yet even with my power, nothing seemed to change.

"Around the same time as my existential crisis, an illness was moving throughout Penrose. Spreading like wildfire, it took the lives of many of my dear comrades. As I helplessly watched my friends die around me, this time not from bullets or explosives, it suddenly came to me. We were making no progress against Tessera because our thought process was all wrong. Just like how a disease kills from within, so should we.

"Instead of attacking from the outside, to finally win we needed to poison them from the inside. My infiltration plan was universally agreed upon, and it was quickly set into motion.

"So, about five years ago I captured, interrogated, and then killed the original Melissa M. Meli, who was being transferred to this facility as an instructor. I stole her identity and, with some help, infiltrated seamlessly right into the heart of Tessera.

"It was extremely difficult to hide among my most hated enemies, but I persevered and did my job faithfully, all in the name of revenge.

"Years went by, and I proved to be invaluable as a spy and saboteur. Being a teacher also gave me some special privileges. On top of access to sensitive information, I had the unique ability to influence the young minds that would soon become the future of Tessera . . . one such as yourself.

"You might imagine that, after so many years of being one of the sheep, I would grow attached to the people here. Ha! You could not be more wrong. I hate these people and this place more than I ever thought possible.

"The people here are nothing but evil. Every time I speak to one of them all I can see are the faces of those who denied my father and me our basic right to life and happiness. The pride and privilege of the people here make me sick; they know nothing of the real world.

"If I could, I would burn this entire place to the ground with everyone in it. The only people who I would even consider saving would be the children, and that is only because they have yet to do anything wrong."

Leo was rendered speechless by Ms. Meli's words, seething with so much hatred and rage. He could almost feel the heat burning his own skin. Never would he have been ready for such a tragic story, especially from the woman who, up until recently, was the sickliest, most upbeat, and quirky person he knew. If her story were just a lie, Leo would have to applaud her sheer creativity, but on the flip side, he dared not think about the repercussions of it being the truth.

7

BREAKING AND ENTERING

AFTER MAKING SMOOTH PROGRESS through the tight vent shaft, Lily came to a sudden halt in the cramped vent, and Locke collided face first right into Lily's hard pack.

"Ouch! Why did you stop so suddenly! Give me a warning next time before you do that!"

Locke listened for a reply, but there was none. He tried to look around the comically large backpack to see the reason for the abrupt stop, to little avail. It was only after a few moments of rubbing his nose that he heard Lily's faint, unenthusiastic voice.

"I see . . . So that's what those symbols meant. Ugh, this is gonna be difficult." She wasn't so much addressing Locke as she was talking to herself. Wriggling herself into a better position, she turned to Locke with a worried expression. "That symbol . . . I know what it means now. Here, take out the map and I'll show you."

Locke took out the map and handed it to her. He held his flashlight over it and listened quietly to her explanation.

"Are you kidding me. . . Lasers? And machine guns! In a ventilation shaft? Who thought that was a good idea?!?"

He thought that just scaling the elevator shafts was bad

enough, but now they had to get past a field of lasers that triggered deadly machine gun turrets.

"If they are the same kind I'm familiar with, my RATS should be able to get around the lasers and disable the turrets momentarily . . . hopefully. If they are built similarly to the ones that guard the command centers."

Locke internally crossed his fingers as he anxiously watched Lily reach into her bag and retrieve her tiny little robotic companions.

They could normally be called semicute, but in the dim light of the small horizontal shaft, they looked more like tiny monsters. Lily took them out one by one and set them on the floor of the shaft. When they were all assembled, they each gave a disciplined squeak, as if saying they were ready for orders.

Lily then reached back inside of her bag and retrieved a small computer screen. As she powered it on, a small picture of each RAT was displayed. Next to each picture was what looked like a status bar and some other detailed charts.

Silently looking on, Locke was impressed. Lily worked with the speed and skill of a master as she programmed a specific task for each RAT.

When she finished, each RAT promptly scurried away to their designated location. The sounds of their tiny metallic feet echoed off the metal walls.

"Hopefully they don't run into their fuzzy alter egos," Lily said as the last robotic rat turned and headed down the ventilation shaft. "I would hate it if they had to fight each other. Not that it would be much of a fight."

She motioned for Locke to move closer. Positioning the screen between them, they monitored the RATS' progress.

"First they need to find the laser field and then find a route through it," Lily said. "Then they need to locate the control box somewhere beyond the lasers and crack into it without setting off the alarm system.

"I've programmed them to cut and splice the correct wires to trick the turret system into forcing a permanent all-clear signal. It would have been much easier to just deactivate the whole system but doing that would alert the security forces; then getting onto the floor would be all but impossible."

It was a tricky plan with many places where things could go terribly wrong, but the reward was much greater than the risk.

"Oh, it looks like Mr. Scruffles made it to the laser field first. I'm gonna take over and put him in manual mode now."

Locke shook his head. *She's named all of them too. At least she's consistent.*

Lily pressed a few buttons on the screen and the view changed. It now showed only the one RAT in the corner of the screen, and now taking up the majority was what looked like a real-time video feed coming from Mr. Scruffles's perspective.

"Hmm, ok. I think I understand the layout now."

From the small screen it could be seen that the vent shaft they were in became gradually large enough to stand up in. Towards the opposite end of the room however, there were what appeared to be small hatches in the ceiling.

Lily pointed at the screen. "See those hatches over there? Those are where the turrets drop down from. You can't see them now, but once something passes through the laser field, living or not, it triggers them to drop down, shredding anything in the space."

"Hmm, so this is where they make the cafeteria's Swiss cheese, huh? I always knew it tasted slightly of gunpowder."

Lily shook her head, but she was smiling. Locke considered even a slight dent in her serious expression a win. Even in a tense situation like this, humor could do wonders to momentarily lift all the pressure riding on their shoulders.

"I'll add comedy lessons to the list then, because that was truly awful."

With Locke's pride in utter shambles, he returned his attention back to the screen. "If those are the turrets, then where are the lasers? I don't see them anywhere."

"Just watch and learn."

Lily's fingers then began to work their magic, as she furiously inputted commands on the screen.

The RAT's tail began to brush the ground near its feet. As its tail gained more speed it began unsettling all the dust and other particles that had gathered in the rather dirty vent system.

Rubbing the ground near his own leg, Locke realized how truly filthy the vents were. Once they finally got out of here, he knew that they would be caked in dust and dirt. After all this excitement, the two of them would definitely need a nice, long soak. Locke longingly sighed at the thought of relaxing in a nice warm bath.

As dust that the RAT had stirred up began to obscure the view of the area, both struggled to see anything on the small screen. Eventually, faint lines began to manifest, traversing the entirety of the seemingly empty space.

"There are so many . . . more than I thought, but I think we can manage."

Lily turned to the astonished Locke, his mouth hanging open.

There were lasers covering every square inch of the entire room, so many he could not even begin to count them. On top of the sheer number, they seemed to disappear and then reappear in completely different positions every few seconds. "Whatever you say."

They both sat there in silence as they tried to come up with some semblance of a strategy to tackle the mountain of a task before them.

"Couldn't we try to reflect the lasers and redirect them around the area we need to get through?"

Lily looked down in thought and shook her head. "No that won't work. Even if we managed to reflect the beams, they are randomly changing locations, and I don't think I could create a program to follow the pattern in such a short time."

"I wish we could just teleport around them," Locke said. "It would make this a whole lot easier."

Unbeknownst to Locke, that simple phrase sparked a chain reaction in Lily's mind.

"Hmm . . . Teleport around them you say . . ." She brought her hand to her chin. "If it's too difficult to go straight through them, maybe we could just go around. Let me see the map again."

Slowly understanding what she had implied, Locke scrambled to retrieve the map.

"Ok, so here we are," he said, "and here's where Mr. Scruffles is. On this map it shows only one way to reach the forty-seventh floor from this direction. But I have an idea. Normally there are many ways to get to every floor. I thought it was strange that this whole vent system only had one specific route, and the fact that it is guarded so heavily seems a little suspicious. It's almost like they want people to come this way . . . like it's a trap, and this map is the bait.

"So now I'm going to change my way of thinking and assume that this map was designed to mislead us. Honestly, that would be totally something I would do. If I frame it that way, it would be an easy way to catch spies.

"Now, using that new assumption, we should try to use your other RATS to find if there are any routes that aren't shown that could possibly go around the laser field."

Lily was looking at him with a strange expression. "Uh . . . s-sure, that sounds like what I was thinking, but I only thought that the map was incomplete. I never would have thought of something so crafty as a setup created by persons unknown. However, the more I think about it, the more it seems plausible."

With this new assumption factored in, Lily began to give out new instructions to her other RATS to scurry throughout the vents. It didn't take long for them to find a few clues that indicated the map they had was indeed wrong. They found slightly newer shafts close to the older one where Locke and Lily were located.

"Ah, so we were right. This map was a trap. Look at all these new vents. If someone came here using this map without the little guys we brought, they would have starved to death in here."

Lily oozed with pride as Locke complimented her creations.

With the help of their tiny robotic friends, they managed to find and trace a path that bypassed the field of lasers. It was too tiny for a person to traverse but perfect for the robotic RATS.

After the RATS rewired the control system for the lasers and turrets, Lily and Locke simply walked right past them. Their goal now seemed within their grasp as they reached the locked grate that would serve as their entry point to the maximum-security floor.

"All right, so now are we going to send the RATS down to scout out the floor?" Locke said, but to his dismay Lily shook her head and pointed.

"I wish we could, but look there."

His gaze followed her finger, and he peered through the holes in the grate at a small box on the nearest wall.

"See that? That's an electromagnetic sensor. It records and tracks all signals going in and out of this floor. My RATS give off a pretty strong signal, and their ID code isn't in the facility's main computer yet, since they haven't gone into production. If we let them go in, they would be flagged as unknown intruders, and the alarms would be triggered instantly."

In other words, their only option was to drop down themselves and find their way to the transmitter without being discovered. Easier said than done.

· · ·

"It seems your friends are taking their sweet time. One third of their time is already spent." As she looked up from her watch, Ms. Meli shrugged nonchalantly. "A fate worse than being shot will await all of us if they don't manage to speed things up."

She made eye contact with Leo and sighed a long, tired sigh. "Spit it out already. It looks like your brain is about to burst with all the questions you have for me. Was my tale that interesting to you? It's sad, but I know many who have had a much harder time than even I."

Leo tried to consolidate his own thoughts, but they were a

jumbled mess. However, there was one question, a simple question, that had reverberated in his mind ever since she had confessed she was not the real Ms. Meli.

"Wh-what is your real name?"

After she realized what he had just asked, a longer than average silence filled the room. Leo had wondered if he had made her angry by asking such a personal question, but to his surprise the opposite occurred.

She raised her free hand to cover a small smile, and a faint, original-style Ms. Meli giggle could be heard as it escaped past her lips.

"My, my, my . . . Of all the questions you could have asked, I never would have thought it would be one so funny. So, you wish to know my real name? It has been many years since I have gone by that name. Becoming a spy, one learns to trivialize such things as simple as a birth name. Hmm, I guess I could tell you now that we are accomplices, but I want to hear your reason for asking first."

Shocked at the nature of her response, Leo's mind went blank. He honestly had no real reason why that question had even escaped his lips, but the more he thought, the more a single answer stuck out.

"I was just curious what I should call you now . . . since you aren't the Ms. Meli I thought you were. It just feels wrong calling you that, now that I know you killed the real one and are just acting in her place."

In response to his simple answer her faint giggle morphed into full-blown laughter. "As I should have expected from a boy like you. So very noble indeed. I guess what you say is indeed true, so being true to my word I shall tell you. The name that was given to me by my mother and father is Sarah . . . Sarah Cooper."

She spoke the words slowly, as if savoring the memories that they brought with them. "You may call me Sarah if you wish; there's no need to stand on ceremony at this point." She said this while looking down at the gun still clutched in her hand. "If all goes well after today, we will never see each other again."

A strong knocking sounded on the door to the apartment, loud enough that it made Leo flinch from surprise. Sarah's eyes narrowed into slits. The knocking continued as Sarah quickly stood up, moving herself into a position where she would not be seen from the doorway. She waved her gun at the door and nodded to Leo, silently telling him to open it.

Leo could feel the tension in the room increase with each step as he walked over to the door. He took a deep breath, wondering if it would be his last, and opened the door with a pained smile.

"What took you so long, Melis—"

The annoyed voice that greeted Leo was cut short as the door fully opened. A middle-aged woman, Mrs. Blum, stood in the doorway with her hands on her hips. Everyone from the academy called her the enemy of fun.

"Oh . . . Leo. What are you doing here? Where is Melissa?"

"I'm sorry," Leo said. "I was told to give Ms. Meli some paperwork from the director. It seems he wants to push through our graduation early, and Ms. Meli needed to sign the paperwork as soon as possible. So right now, she is in her office making sure everything is in order."

Leo managed to sound calm, even despite the fact that a gun was trained on both of them. He knew that if either of them made the slightest mistake, they would both be gunned down without any hesitation. He figured the only reason he seemed so calm was the mixture of getting used to a gun being pointed at him and the fact that he was mostly telling the truth, albeit missing some details.

At the mere mention of the director, the expression on Mrs. Blum's face changed instantly. That was how much sheer influence the director had over the facility's residents.

"Oh, if the director sent you at this time of day, he must have something important planned. I'm only here to give these student files to Ms. Meli; she forgot them in the classroom today. You didn't hear this from me, but I swear that girl would forget her own head if it wasn't attached to her body."

She gave a weary smile and held out a small bundle of files. "If you would be so kind, could you bring these to her? Tell her I need them finished before the next class period; she'll understand. But before I forget—congratulations! Today sure has been an exciting day for you and the other two."

Leo took the files and thanked her. She waved as Leo closed the door. He slid to the ground. It felt as though his heart was going to beat straight out of his chest.

Sarah stepped closer to him, still on alert for noises coming from outside. "To be honest I always hated that woman. Too bad I couldn't tell her how I really felt about her. Get up. We can't stay here any longer. I can't risk any more uninvited guests coming to disturb us."

Reaching the doorway, she took a jacket that was hanging by the door and put it on.

"If I remember correctly, you mentioned that those two would be entering the forty-seventh floor from your secret base, correct? I have a feeling no one will bother us there. Get up!

You're going to take me there; we can also meet up with your little friends when they are done."

She lightly kicked Leo, who was still doubled over on the ground. As he got his nerves under control, Leo looked up at her and nodded. Although he didn't like it, taking her there was the best option to not only meet back up with Locke and Lily but also to avoid getting anyone else involved.

Slowly standing, Leo watched Sarah place her pistol in her jacket pocket.

"Don't get any funny ideas. Just because you can't see it, doesn't mean I still can't shoot you."

After making sure there were no sounds of footsteps outside the door, the two quietly exited the apartment, Leo in front of what appeared to be Ms. Meli, lazily strolling behind him with her hands in her pockets.

• • •

With two light thuds, Lily and Locke dropped down from the vent onto the forbidden forty-seventh floor. Luckily, the vent was above a small recess off the main corridor. Quickly trying to get their bearings and making sure that no one was around, Lily's eyes focused on Locke's form.

"Wipe yourself off," she said, in a hushed voice. "You're covered in dust. We can't go leaving literal footprints for them to track us."

Locke could only shake his head and point back at her. She was caked in so much dirt that it looked as if she had just been the first person to crawl through a ventilation system that was a few decades old.

"Fine, fine . . . I get it," she said.

Locke quickly managed to clean himself off and hide the evidence, but Lily was having some difficulty. She had removed all the dirt from her shoes, but the grime was almost permanently fused with her clothes. She sighed in disgust and joined Locke, who had been keeping watch.

They peeked around the corner into what appeared to be one of the main hallways. To their relief, no one was in the hall, and they briskly walked around the corner, trying to stick as close as possible to the wall.

"Which way is the transmitter?" Lily whispered to Locke. "Are you sure it's this way?"

He indicated ahead of them. "According to the map, there's a big junction up ahead, which should mean a floor diagram. I think I know which way to go, but if there is one, we could check it out."

Just as Locke said, after a few seconds of failing to be as stealthy as they would have liked, they reached the hallway junction. It was a rather large four-way intersection, and placed in the dead center was a kiosk with a large screen.

Peering around the strangely empty open area, Locke debated whether it would be worth the risk to run out and quickly look at the screen. Just as he decided against it however, a booming, static-filled voice interrupted his train of thought.

"Attention all personnel. Code sixty-three has been put into effect. All nonsecurity staff are required to exit the floor. Again, code sixty-three is in effect."

Turning to each other, Lily and Locke exchanged a look of confusion and spoke the same question. "Do you know what code sixty-three is?" They both simultaneously shook their heads.

"Ugh, if only Leo were here," Lily said. "I'm sure he would know. He did spend all that time studying those protocol and code books that we found that one time."

Locke could only begrudgingly agree, although if Leo were here with them, then there wouldn't be any need for them to be here sneaking around in the first place. "Since we don't know what that code means, should we just play it safe and assume they know about us? Which means we really need to find the fastest way there. Stay here and keep watch."

Against his better judgment Locke took a deep breath, quickly scanned the empty intersection, and then sprinted towards the kiosk and skidded to a halt in front of it. Attempting to decipher the floor diagram was difficult. It had many paths that went every which way, marked with strange symbols for good measure. It was almost as if whoever designed this system had really hated their job, so as payback, they created this device as some sort of cruel joke.

Finally finding his bearings, Locke skimmed the long list of rooms until he found the communications center. Then looking back up at the map, he traced the fastest route from their current location.

To Locke, it seemed that he and Lily were currently in the focal point of the four hallways on this floor. Between them and the communication center was the military prototype testing area, medical research area, and a facility break room. Doing a bit of mental calculation Locke realized that, if they tried to avoid all those places, it would take a significant amount of time.

Their best option would be to detour through one of the less crowded areas in their path and then exit on the other side. But which area offered the best chance to go undetected?

Returning to Lily's side, he described the map in detail to her and told her his plan to save time.

"Hmm . . . I see your point. That probably is the best option. If we choose correctly, it might give us some cover as we move towards the communication center. We should head in that direction first and see if we run into anyone else before we pick which area to cut through. Honestly, I have a weird feeling. I can't believe we haven't seen a single person yet."

Locke nodded in agreement, and they cautiously continued down the corridor. The first area that branched from their current path was the prototype testing area. Preparing to peek around the corner, Lily and Locke heard a soft rustling mixed with the mechanical sounds of hydraulics, followed by a tremendous rushing sound. It almost sounded as if there were a high-pressure water hose operating somewhere nearby. As they strained to listen, the strange sounds abruptly stopped.

As Locke quickly exchanged a look with Lily, the sound began again, louder. Much louder. The sound was coming from something massive directly around the corner, mere feet from their position. Locke had no idea what could be coming from the advanced testing area, but that didn't matter; they could not afford to be spotted.

They turned and ran as far as they could from the intimidating noise, only stopping when they reached the medical area. Doubled over, trying to catch their breath, they again tried to listen for the sounds of anyone inside.

Locke was sure there were no robotic sounds inside. The only thing he heard for sure was the furious pounding of his own heart.

"I don't hear anything. This might be our best chance for cutting through. It should have a lot of stuff we can use for cover and not nearly as many people as the break rooms."

After stabilizing her own breathing, Lily agreed, and they quietly entered the first room of the medical area.

They hugged the wall, moving quickly. Row after row of large vertical tanks filled with all kinds of substances neatly stretched the entire length of the room. Lining the perimeter of the room were glowing computer screens and controls. To Locke, the tanks almost resembled rows of soldiers at attention. It was oddly satisfying to look at.

Edging their way around the perimeter of the room, a hypnotic beeping that one often heard in a medical facility was the only sound. A faint glow emanated from each tank. As they reached about a third of the way through the room, two voices could be heard approaching from the doorway on the opposite side of the room.

"So, there was another code sixty-three again. What is that, the third time this week?"

"Uh, yeah. It's almost like those guys at the top have no idea what we have to go through every time they force us to shut everything down."

"At least we're almost done. This is the last room, right? Then we can finally go home."

As the voices got closer, Locke and Lily frantically looked for a place to hide. All they could do was to crouch down and comically hide behind two of the large tanks.

Peeking around the tank he was hiding behind, Locke saw two individuals in lab coats, walking down an aisle between the tanks. Their voices sounded irritated as they continued to the center of the room and stopped at one of the tanks.

"Tank forty-five, stage two. Seems to be progressing smoothly. There's good development in the extremities, and brain activity seems to be strong. It's such a shame we have to shut this beauty down."

"Yeah, this one is by far the best of the batch. Eighty-four over there isn't even responsive to external stimuli yet. It pains me to have to pull the plug on one so promising . . . but orders are orders."

As Lily and Locke continued to listen in from behind their tanks, the conversation of the two men only served to pique Locke's curiosity more. He noticed that one of the men was operating a handheld computer.

"All right, I'll pull the plug now. It should take a few hours until termination is complete. We should pass by the custodians on the way out and let them know that these tanks will need to be decontaminated in time for the next batch."

The two men then quickly headed towards the door that Locke and Lily had just entered from. They could only press themselves tightly against their tanks and pray that they would not be noticed as the men walked past. As the two men's footsteps grew fainter, Lily peeked her head out and scanned the room.

"I think they are finally gone."

Slowly, Lily stood up. Her eyes widened as she felt an invisible hand tightly grip her stomach.

Inside the tank, meeting her gaze at eye level was not an animal like she had guessed from the two men's conversation. Instead, it was something else that resembled something very familiar.

"L-L-Locke. Look in the tank! There's something in the tank!!! There's a baby in the tank . . ." Lily had forgotten to whisper. Her eyes widened as she frantically tried to get Locke's attention.

"Shhh! What are y—"

Locke was stunned. Inside the tank he was crouched behind mere seconds before was a small baby boy floating helplessly in the unknown fluid of the tank. As he wordlessly looked closer, he could see that there were many tubes connected to the baby's body. It also looked to have an expression of discomfort frozen on its tiny face.

Locke wasn't even aware that he had started to talk, his mouth moving all on its own. "Why are they doing this? Why are there babies here???"

"M-maybe they need to be in these tanks? On the screens over there it looks like they are tracking their vital signs."

Lily pointed to one of the many monitors.

Looking at the screens, she was probably right. This was a medical facility within Tessera, after all; it was probably just some form of advanced medical treatment.

"You're probably right, medical care does sometimes seem rather dangerous and strange to someone who is untrained. We should just get moving."

Locke turned away from the baby in the tank, grabbed Lily's hand, and started to walk towards the door that the two men had come through, the whole while trying to shut out the mysterious words the men had said right before they had left. What did they mean by "pulling the plug"?

As he repeated the phrase over and over again in his mind, they passed tank after tank. Each was filled with a baby bigger than the last; the tanks seemed to be set up in order of age, from youngest to oldest.

Knowing that Lily would stop and stare every chance she got, he held tightly onto her hand as they walked. However, just as they were about to reach the next doorway, Lily came to a sudden halt.

"Lily, come on . . . We can't waste anymore time." He turned, expecting her to be staring at the baby in the tank, but her intense expression and focus still took him off guard. "Why are you staring at that one?"

To Locke, it seemed no different than the rest, albeit much larger. Honestly, this particular one couldn't really even be called a baby anymore.

Lily was transfixed as her lips began to part. Only growing more confused as he watched her struggling to form words, Locke suddenly became aware that her hand, which was still clasped within his own, was trembling.

"What is it? Come on te—"

"This baby . . .This baby looks exactly like you . . ."

"What do you mean?"

"It's face . . . It looks just like yours only smaller."

Lily spoke without breaking her gaze away from the tank. A terrible feeling of dread welled up in the pit of Locke's stomach as he stepped closer to the tank. Locke was surprised he had not noticed it earlier; the resemblance was uncanny. As they both stared at the boy floating within the tank, it began to stir.

"Look . . . What is it doing??" Lily said, just as the baby seemed to have noticed their presence. It began to slowly move about in the tank. As if attracted to the sounds of their voices, it moved from the middle of the tank towards them.

"It seems like it heard us."

Whenever Locke would speak, the baby's expression seemed to subtly change, its once frozen expression becoming somewhat softer.

"It seems to like you," Lily said as she pushed Locke closer to the tank.

Locke had no idea what to make of it. Finding a baby in a tank that looked exactly like him? Not to mention it was within the most secret area of the entire facility. He already had a million questions piling up. Locke felt that at any moment there would be an avalanche within his own mind, and he would be quickly buried beneath the weight of all the questions. What finally brought him back to reality was the girl beside him.

As Locke was being buried alive, Lily, on the other hand, was desperately trying to play with the child. She had started to make silly faces and hand gestures from her side of the glass. All in order to get the same response that Locke's voice had just produced.

"What are you doing?" he asked, already knowing the answer.

"It's not fair that you made it happy. I wanna make it happy toooo! It's not fair . . ."

Childish jealousy could be heard in her voice, but she winked at him. It made Locke feel a little bit lighter just knowing that, even in a situation like this one, Lily was still just as goofy and fun-loving as she always was.

Locke gave a long sigh. "Well, it looks like it's working. But I still think he likes me better . . . especially because, if that baby really is me, it must have good taste."

Lily looked at him in slight irritation and puffed out her cheeks, mimicking the baby.

The baby, who this whole time had been watching intently,

looked on as if it found their banter amusing. It raised one of its small arms and pointed, however it was not pointing at either of the two of them. Lily was the first to notice its gesture.

"Look . . . I think it wants to show us something."

Locke followed the path of the little finger, which led to another tank in the adjacent row. Just when he thought that there couldn't be anything else that would surprise him, his mouth dropped open.

"That one looks . . . It looks just like you, Lily . . . And that one in the row next to it . . . It looks just like Leo!"

He ran towards the row where the baby Locke had been pointing. He rubbed his eyes to make sure they were not deceiving him. Locke began to run down the entire length of the room. At that moment all thought of being stealthy was out the window. As he ran down the rows, it became all too clear. Each row held baby versions of either Leo, Lily, or himself. From one end of the room to the other the ages increased, from extremely tiny embryos to some who looked to be about one to two years old. It was utterly astounding.

As Locke returned to Lily's side, it seemed she had also come to grasp the true intentions of this mysterious room. Just as she was about to speak, however, voices could be heard emanating from the hallway outside the entrance.

"I think I heard someone running in the lab over there. Shouldn't Dr. Nest and the others have gone home by now?"

At the sounds of approaching footsteps, the two looked at each other and then at the door leading to the communication center. Having no time to talk about what they had just seen, they hurried to the next room.

They made their way in silence through some vacant smaller rooms filled with examining tables and medical equipment. Locke wanted to talk about what they had just seen, but he was too unwilling to be the first person to bring it up.

After traveling in silence and making sure they were not being followed, they reached the entrance to the communication area. It looked to be the smallest area that the two had seen so far, consisting of three little rooms. They peeked around the corner and, deciding it was safe, walked into the first room.

"All right," Locke said. "We need to find the transmitter; you go in that room, and I'll look in this room."

Lily nodded and sneaked into the next room.

Taking a good look around, Locke realized that he had no idea what he was looking for. He had never seen a long-range transmitter before. He assumed it would have some sort of microphone or headphones connected to it. He just hoped he would recognize it when he saw it.

Finding nothing promising, he walked into the last room and stopped. In the middle of the room stood a large machine. Noticing Lily enter, Locke said, "I think I found it. This thing is massive; how far do you think it can reach?"

"It's easily taller and wider than both of us put together," Lily said. "So this is what she meant by long-range transmitter. Even this deep within the facility it could probably communicate with old space satellites. No wonder it's kept on this floor. This thing is probably worth more than the cost of outfitting an entire army."

Lily's love of all thing's technology was abundantly on display. She didn't even attempt to suppress it as she ogled the monstrous piece of technology. Locke couldn't help but shake his head at his companion.

"Geez," he said. "We don't have the time to play with this thing all day." Reaching into his bag, he retrieved the message that they were told to transmit. He handed the envelope to Lily, and she walked up to the transmitter's rather small console.

"I hope whatever is in this message is really that important," Lily said as she furiously began to type on the keyboard. "This thing is sure old and slow; I could make so many improvements if I had all my tools here."

Right as she hit her last keystroke the transmitter hummed to life.

"All right, I entered the frequency that was written on the envelope. Now I'm just going to scan the message into the system; then we should be good to go."

Lily opened the letter and then pushed it inside of a small slit that Locke had not noticed before. As the machine slowly ate the paper, Lily took off her backpack and rummaged inside. Once the paper was out of sight, Lily stood up and, from within her large pack, withdrew two blocks of C-4.

"You really plan on using those? What the heck is wrong with you? You're gonna kill us both!"

"Don't be overdramatic," Lily said as she placed both her hands, which were still holding the explosives, on her hips. "I'm gonna use a remote detonator, remember? She told us to sabotage it and then leave the bag we brought as evidence."

Locke waved his arms in defeat. "Fine, fine. Do what you want. But I'm going to stand waaay over there while you set it up." He watched from the safety of the corner of the room and sighed.

It only took the skilled hands of Lily a few moments to wire the whole transmitter to blow. It now reminded Locke of stories he had been told about things called "Christmas trees," with all the bright wires and shapes hanging every which way. Although he never remembered any stories where the Christmas tree exploded at the end.

8

DEVELOPMENTS

"WE DON'T HAVE MUCH TIME LEFT,**"** Locke said, as he looked down at his watch. "I hope Ms. Meli's poor time management wasn't just an act."

As they raced to return to the opened ventilation shaft that would lead to their salvation, Locke did some rough mental calculations. At their current rate they would only be able to make it back to their hideout before time ran out. Locke mentally kicked himself for wasting so much time on their journey.

Lily shrugged. "Don't worry; we can make it in time. It's much easier to climb down then to climb up these elevator shafts. Also, I have a feeling that she wouldn't do anything, even if we were a little late. She needs us after all. Without confirmation that we succeeded with our mission she's just as trapped as we are. I don't think she's dumb enough to try anything crazy while there is still a good possibility of escape."

Locke was quietly taken off guard by Lily's calm and rational train of thought. He couldn't help but feel that, during this adventure, their usual roles had been reversed. He liked to view himself as the distant and calculating type, but this time he felt more emotionally driven and not nearly as calm as he was before.

Maybe he was changing. He looked back at Lily. *Maybe both of us are changing.*

Although Lily still shone bright with her usual quirkiness, it seemed different than it had in the past, almost as if her old silliness was serving a new purpose. Locke couldn't quite put his finger on it.

Watching Lily comically struggle to climb back up into the ventilation shaft, Locke sighed. Maybe he was just overthinking it.

After both were safely within the shaft, Lily pulled out the detonator she had shown Locke while they were still in the communication center. A large, childlike grin spread across her face as Locke covered his ears and closed his eyes.

Not knowing what to expect, Locke slightly opened his eyes and peered at Lily. All he managed to see was her mouth appear to make the word "Boom" as, without hesitation, she flipped the switch. At that same instant, a terrific sound could be heard reverberating throughout the entire floor.

He had never been in the proximity of an explosion before. But what shocked him the most, besides the deafening sound, was the sheer concussive force that assaulted his chest. It was simultaneously thrilling and terrifying. However, just as his hearing returned, a new sound battered his ears.

As expected, the explosion attracted a bit of attention. Mere seconds after the effects of the explosion had subsided, all the alarms on the entire floor were triggered. Even within the vent system, the sound of the alarm system and the rushing of feet could still be heard.

Retracing their path through the shaft, the noises from the commotion began to become less noticeable. This relieved

Locke. It didn't seem like they were following them in the vent system, at least.

Further down the shaft, they finally met back up with their tiny ratlike companions. Upon laying eyes on them Lily could hardly contain herself out of sheer joy. She picked each one up and hugged them close, just as one would do after reuniting with a long-lost family pet. Despite the fact that she was clutching metallic RATS in her arms, the sight was adorable.

Locke watched her closely and couldn't help smiling. Even with her own life in danger, Lily still considered the well-being of her creations. "Lily, why do you care so much about your robots? It's not like they're alive or anything."

"I've been expecting either you or Leo to ask that," she said, placing the little creatures into her pack. "It's honestly pretty simple. I know my life is temporary, but these creations of mine don't have a definite lifespan like we do. So, by creating them, I try to put a small piece of myself within each one of them. Whether it be a small dream or goal of mine, all the things I create hold a piece of me. So even after I die, I hope that at least some of my babies will remain. As long as they remain, the pieces of me that I placed within them will live on. Then I can, by proxy, continue to affect the world after my body has long since disappeared. *Wellll*, that's how I feel anyways . . . It's kind of hard to explain."

Locke tilted his head in confusion. He had never expected such a thought-out response from her. He could understand caring about something that one had put great effort into creating, but to continue to affect the world after one had died? He could not help feeling baffled as he watched Lily continue to pack up like nothing of importance had just happened.

"I know it's hard to put into words, but I think everyone strives to leave an impact on the world," she said. "In this case, mine is to create my inventions. You might not have realized yours yet. But when you do, I think you'll truly understand what I mean."

Locke nodded, but the more he thought about it, maybe he already knew what his goal in life was. Unlike Lily, whose goal was to put pieces of herself into her various creations, he had been subconsciously placing himself within his two friends. Instead of putting his thoughts and feelings into something he could create, Locke was sharing his thoughts and feelings with his two best friends. So even after he eventually did die, all the best parts of himself, his thoughts and feelings, would always live on in them. All it took was Lily and her tiny robotic RATS for him to realize it. So far on this journey he had felt tiny bits of it, but now those feelings had matured and evolved before his very eyes. Locke had gained a purpose.

Locke would place pieces of himself within his two best friends and only allies. He would protect and help them reach their own dreams. It all finally made sense to him, and he felt a surge of drive as they approached the entrance to their base. It hadn't been more than an hour, but he desperately wanted to see Leo. He just hoped he was ok.

As if reading his expression, Lily spoke up in a reassuring voice. "He'll be just fine; he's stronger than the two of us, after all."

She finally opened the last grate to enter the base. However, it wasn't just the bright light from inside the room that greeted them. A familiar voice could be heard as they crawled through the opening, but it wasn't the voice of the one Locke so badly wanted to see.

"What took you two so long? You're late you know. You're lucky I didn't keep my word and shoot your friend here. Since you came back, can I assume you completed your mission, at the very least?"

Ms. Meli casually sat on the bed in the middle of Lily's once private room, while Leo sat cross legged on the floor beside her. Upon seeing Lily and Locke, however, a big smile crossed his face as he jumped to his feet.

Both Lily and Locke cried out simultaneously. "Leo!"

At their tandem cry, Leo rushed over to his two friends. "Lily! Locke! You guys! You guys . . . look awful."

Caught slightly off guard, Lily and Locke looked at each other and then broke down into laughter. "I guess we do look a little ragged," Locke said. "I swear I'm never going to climb around in vents ever again!" This was only met with more laughter.

"You know, you already said that earlier today. At this rate, you'll just jinx yourself again," Leo said, smiling.

An unpleasant voice, teeming with sarcasm, cut through the joyous air. "Not to break up this wonderfully touching reunion, but I need some answers." Ms. Meli menacingly waved her gun in the trio's direction. "First things first. Did you send the message? Spit it out already; we don't have much time if you triggered the alarms."

Leo turned back to his companions, looking eager to hear their response as well. Lily shyly turned her head. Locke sighed as he racked his brain on how to properly answer while, at the same time, keeping some semblance of an advantage over their adversary.

Seeing the impatience grow on Leo's and, more importantly,

Ms. Meli's face, Locke quickly and vaguely described the events that had transpired.

The two listened intently. Every once in a while, Lily who was getting more comfortable, chimed in with some extraneous details. Locke told them about the maze of ventilation shafts and how they had discovered that the map they had was most likely a trap designed to mislead spies.

He told them how they had managed to circumnavigate the lasers and entered the forty-seventh floor, as well as briefly describing the floor's layout, which he had memorized from the directional signs on the floor itself.

When he got to the point in the story where they had made their way through the testing area, Lily enthusiastically took over.

"After we managed to run away from the robot in the experimental testing center, we headed through the medical area. While there, we did run into some people, but we managed to not get seen. But you'll never guess what we saw in there!"

Locke gave her a swift elbow to her ribs, without Ms. Meli noticing. Thankfully, Lily got the message, but her enthusiasm had piqued the interest of both Leo and Ms. Meli. They both leaned forward, expecting to hear something of great significance.

"In . . . In the lab we saw . . . We saw tons of cute animals! They had all these adorable puppies and kittens in cages. It was so sad. I wanted to pet and play with them sooo bad!"

Leo, Locke, and Ms. Meli all just blinked in disbelief, albeit for completely different reasons. Locke again took the reins of the conversation, just as Ms. Meli's expression became more agitated.

"I apologize for her, Ms. Meli. She can get a little distracted. So, after that we had no trouble finding the communication center and the transmitter. We sent the message on the designated frequency, then rigged the whole thing to blow and planted that evidence you told us to leave at the scene. As we fled back through the vents, we detonated the explosives, which triggered all the alarms on that floor. They should still be scrambling to figure everything out as we speak."

"Call me Sarah. There's no need for me to go by 'Ms. Meli' anymore. Leo here can explain my little situation to you after we get out of this awful place."

Leo nodded in response, and she said, "At the present I think we'll be safe from suspicion, especially when they find that little present you left for them. However, we still need to remain vigilant and proceed under the assumption that we are being watched from now on. The news that the map I had acquired was possibly a trap definitely concerns me. I will be looking into that matter as soon as possible. However, our first objective at this point is to return to our daily lives as if nothing has happened."

She stowed her gun away, and her serious demeanor seemed to relax just a tiny bit.

"I will return to being the teacher that you once knew, and you three will continue to be the annoying students that I have to deal with. Or I suppose now you'll be working for the director. Hmm, interesting . . . That could actually be very good for us. Since now we are true accomplices, I can have you three do a bit of information gathering for me."

• • •

Leo's uneasiness grew. He and his comrades were in quite the predicament. No matter how one looked at it, they were between a rock and hard place. After committing such an act of treason and sabotage, Leo knew that Tessera, especially the colonel, would not forgive them. Even though they were under duress, they would most likely still be executed, if only to be made an example of for other would-be spies. Their destinies were now bound with their once airheaded but now mysterious teacher.

Leo still harbored a great number of suspicions about her and her past. In the end though, he felt that sticking with her would give them the greatest odds of making it out of this situation alive.

She had managed to stay hidden in the facility for so long, after all. She seemed to value her own life and was dedicated to her mission, which was slightly reassuring. Based on her personality, Sarah would hold self-preservation above all else and thus limit her own risk and, by extension, their own.

It might even be possible to somehow escape with her if they were given the chance. He had no idea who she had tried to contact, but it may be possible that someone was coming to get her out.

Interrupting Leo's train of thought, Locke spoke up. "We should all go back to our quarters now. It is getting late, after all, not to mention security is going to be on high alert everywhere. We don't want to get flagged, so it would be safest if we moved before they get any more organized and realize what happened."

The alert was still very fresh, and they could probably make it back to their rooms before the whole facility was under lockdown. Leo also suspected that, by the way both Locke and Lily were acting, they were hiding something from Sarah about what they saw on the forty-seventh floor. "I agree with Locke, we should go back now."

"You have a good point," Sarah said. "All right, let's get out of here, but we shouldn't all leave together, so I will head out first."

The trio followed Sarah back to their original secret base, back through the maze of boxes and past the charging Rusty. Before she climbed into the vent however, she turned to face them. The relaxed expression from a moment ago had vanished.

"I think this place will make a good meeting location. So, whenever I contact you, we should meet here unless otherwise stated . . . Oh and by the way, I'll be keeping a close eye on you three, and if I get the feeling you are going to somehow sabotage me or do anything to get in my way, I will not hesitate to kill all of you. I have many other accomplices within this facility . . . I was not the one responsible for the disturbance earlier."

The trio did not take her threat lightly as they watched her leave the small room. After making sure that Sarah was indeed gone, they all began talking at once.

"You'll never guess . . ."

"So, what was so impor—"

"*WE SAW BABIES!!!!*"

"*HUHH????????*" Leo had expected a few different things, but babies were not among them. "Lily, what do you mean by 'babies'?"

As Lily frantically tried to explain, the only thing Leo managed to understand was that they had, in fact, found live human babies.

After a few painful moments of watching Leo's confused expression grow, Locke was forced to cut in and re-explain everything.

"Ohhh, I think I understand now . . . So, in the medical facility you found what appeared to be baby versions of us inside tanks on the forty-seventh floor, and then you overheard the conversation of the doctors there."

After repeating what he was told, it began to sink in.

"You found clone versions of us inside tanks on the forty-seventh floor?!?" Leo said, too loudly.

He had no idea what to think. If it weren't Lily and Locke telling him this, he wouldn't have believed it, that was how absurd it sounded. The longer Leo listened to their shocking story, the more the gears of his mind began to turn, and he came to a sudden realization. Growing up within the facility, he always had many small nagging questions that no one would ever give him clear answers to.

Before he had ever met his two dear companions, he never had what one would call a family with a father and mother. It was always just himself and one of various facility-appointed caregivers. He remembered always asking them the same simple question. "Why do I not have a mother and father? Everyone else in my class has one. Why don't I?" That childlike question was always met by hesitation and nervous fear.

As one does with a young child asking an awkward question, he was always given the same set of dismissive answers. "You are special," they would say. "Why do you want them; you have us." After a time, he would not even bother to ask. Although it would still weigh heavily on his mind from time to time.

It wasn't until he met Lily and Locke that his questions about his family were truly forgotten about. For the three had clicked the moment they met each other, almost as if they were a perfectly matching set of puzzle pieces. Leo's questions about his family had not resurfaced since then. He now considered Locke and Lily his only family.

But upon hearing what the two had seen, the dam holding back his long-forgotten question broke, and it came flooding back.

Taking a deep breath, Leo spoke about what he had once long since forgotten. "Lily . . . Locke, everything makes sense now . . . It all makes sense now. I didn't want to believe it, but I think each of us knows it's true."

Leo lowered his gaze. He felt as if, speaking his thoughts out loud, there would be no going back. All of their lives up to that point would need to be re-evaluated, everything they had ever done, seen, and been told.

"We are not normal humans. We are probably just one of the many beings you guys saw within those tanks. We are just a Tessera experiment, beings created to be used and, if it is deemed necessary, thrown away and replaced. It all has become so clear to me now, how we have always been treated, the coincidence of us all having no family, our abilities, and especially what happened at the celebration today. I thought we had won an award for being top of our class, but it was something different altogether."

Lily and Locke both seemed to have come to the same conclusion as Leo, and both their faces reflected the inner turmoil that follows having everything you thought you knew flipped on its head. All three stood in a profound silence, in direct conflict with the roaring Leo experienced within the confines of his mind.

A whimpering sound could be heard. Lily looked down at the creature making soft mechanical sounds by her feet. She watched as her creation comically chased his own tail in circles for a few moments and then looked up sadly towards his master, as if apologizing for being unable to catch it. She gave a melancholy smile. "Thank you, Rusty . . . You are a very good boy."

Rusty looked up at her with his mechanical expression and tilted his head as if trying to show concern. It appeared as though her robotic friend had made an expression that transcended cold steel. She crouched down and patted his head and quietly thanked him again. "I'll be sure to fix your eye when all of this is figured out."

Seeming to like the idea, Rusty nodded his metal snout vigorously and licked her hand in approval. Looking to each of her companions in turn, she took a deep breath and said, "It will all be ok."

Locke's troubled expression softened, and he turned to Leo. "She's right, Leo . . . The circumstances don't matter. All that matters is that we are together. I know as long as we're together we can make it through just about anything."

As Leo looked to each of his dear friends, his vision slowly became hazy. He felt a warm sensation envelope his body as the three friends embraced.

"Don't cry, Leo," Lily said.

He hadn't even realized he was crying, but as he returned the warm embrace, he felt a wet tear run down his face.

The trio stayed locked in a three-way embrace for what seemed like forever. All that could be heard were the slight sniffles coming from their tight huddle and the quiet, sympathetic whine of Rusty, as he looked up at them, trapped within the trio's center.

9

DECEPTION

LEO SLOWLY OPENED HIS HEAVY EYES. At the same time, he tried to scooch his body into a sitting position but to little avail, for both of his arms were unresponsive to his commands, gone completely numb from the two lumps currently pinning them to his bed. As he carefully tried to remove his trapped arms from underneath his two sleeping companions, he could hear their soft, consistent breathing finally begin to stir.

It had been a long time since the three of them had fallen asleep like this, together in the same room. In the past it was much more common, especially when Lily or Locke couldn't manage to fall asleep. They would always manage to somehow find a way to sneak into Leo's room, even when he was firmly against it. There had been many times he had gone to sleep alone in his seemingly locked bedroom, only to wake up the next morning surrounded by his two friends, without any memory of them sneaking in.

As Locke stirred and slowly began to wake, Leo, who was still partially trapped under his friend's body, couldn't help reminiscing about those good times. However, in this case, all three of them had chosen to stay together in order to further discuss their situation and make a plan.

Although no one had said it out loud, there was another reason altogether. The three of them simply wanted to stay together.

Similarly to how a young child needs a favorite blanket to sleep at night, they felt safe and secure just knowing each other was nearby.

It seemed to do the trick for both Lily and Locke, who Leo had heard loudly snoring away throughout the whole night. Leo, on the other hand, barely slept a wink. His mind just couldn't help but replay every aspect of recent events. He could not afford to gloss over even a single detail; their future survival depended on not making mistakes.

Thankfully, feeling quickly returned to Leo's arms as his two companions finally awoke and sluggishly began to get ready for the day. Even though it was Leo's room, Lily and Locke pulled some of their extra clothes out of the depths of Leo's closet.

"You do realize this is my closet, right? And my room? Would it kill you guys to not leave your stuff in here all the time?"

Lily smiled at Locke, who said, "Sure . . . Whatever you say, Leo."

Leo just rolled his eyes at them. Before he could berate them further, he heard sudden footsteps outside, and an abrupt knock sounded at the door.

The trio were suddenly on edge, as if they were prey that could sense a predator nearby. They looked at one another with slight panic on their faces. Who could it be this early in the morning? Leo thought that no one could have figured out their involvement so quickly, but that was only a hypothesis.

Locke managed to compose himself first and walked over to the door. He turned to the other two and, forcing a big grin, said,

"Don't worry. Just remember to smile. We are just a bunch of dumb kids, after all." He then opened the door.

"Is that the face you make when you greet your favorite teacher? Creepy," Sarah said, in a sing-song voice. She held a small box in each hand. "Don't worry. I only came to bring you these. You left them in my apartment when you came to drop off that paperwork yesterday."

Although her voice seemed innocent enough, her gaze was a different animal entirely. She looked at the three as if she was a hunter aiming down the scope of her rifle.

It was obvious to Leo that returning what they had forgotten was not the only reason for her early visit. More likely it was to check up on them to see if they had been found out and, if not, to intimidate them just a little bit.

Sarah handed over the items in question to Locke. He managed to keep the same forced smile on his face as he politely thanked her. The two small boxes were the gifts they had received from the director. Leo had completely forgotten about them during all the commotion.

"Don't mention it. I did not open them or anything. Not even I could open a special gift that was meant for someone else . . . although I did admire the wrapping a bit."

Leo knew that if she was even the least bit suspicious of the boxes, she would have made sure to figure out what was in them. But as Locke took the boxes, it appeared what she had told them was the truth, as their wrapping was in perfect condition.

Locke's eyes narrowed and his gaze became more intense. Leo couldn't help but notice the change in Locke's expression. Although he was curious as to what caused it, he remained silent.

Shifting the boxes in his hands, Locke spoke slowly and deliberately. "Thank you for returning these to us. We will be sure not to misplace our things again. But if we do, I am hopeful that you will be able to help us again."

Seeming to get the message that Locke was subtly hinting, Sarah nodded her head, and then just as suddenly as she had appeared, she turned on her heel and walked away. To Leo it had seemed as though, besides speaking a few sentences of little meaning to each other, an entire hidden battle had just taken place between the two.

As Locke closed the door, Leo said, "What was that? Was she giving you a code or something?"

To Leo's surprise, Locke just waved his hand dismissively. "I think you're starting to overthink things a little too much. When she handed me the boxes and mentioned the wrapping, I noticed that she had hidden a message on the underside of one of the boxes, that's all. I assume it's just instructions on our next meeting, so I gave her some sort of affirmative."

He showed the tiny note stuck to the bottom of one of the box's wrapping. Locke peeled it off carefully and opened it. As he was opening the note, Leo and Lily moved over both his shoulders to read it.

My grade book shows that you three haven't finished all your assignments for this quarter yet. Even if the director is summoning you very soon, I feel it is my duty as a proper teacher to formally complete your education. I will be asking you three to be ready for me to drop in every now and again to give you private lessons. Just a fair warning: I won't go easy on you three now that you're moving up in the world. Be sure not to forget all the things I've taught you, and remember, we

are all watching your progress very closely. Your magnificent
teacher, Ms. Melissa M. Meli.

Lily scratched her head as they finished reading the letter. "I don't get it. I thought this was supposed to be some set of instructions or a mission or something."

Locke playfully poked her forehead. "No silly, it's just that she wrote it in a code. She can't just write stuff like that and have it possibly become evidence for the whole world to see. What if someone other than us read it? We would all be killed. Although . . . there are some parts that I don't even fully understand."

Lily pouted in response to Locke's poking, and snatched the letter from his grasp. "I got she wants to disguise our meetings as nothing more than lessons. Plus there is the threat that she will be keeping an eye on us. Although, I don't get what she means about us seeing the director soon."

Leo said, "Hmm, I don't get it eith—"

Another abrupt knock came from the door. It almost made Leo jump; he had not heard any footsteps this time.

"She must have forgotten to tell us something," Lily said. "I'm going to give that lady a piece of my mind." She stormed over to the door and yanked it open. The note Lily had been holding fell slowly to the ground.

"Oh good!" said Sergeant Kyle Briggs. "I was afraid none of you three were going to be in your rooms, but it seems I found you after all. Phew . . . It looks like I've escaped having to receive more 'training.' I have direct orders to have you three follow me to the director's office at once. I was told not to take no for an answer."

Leo had thought he would never see the large sergeant again. As it turned out, fate seemed to be in a mood to see how many times it could prove him wrong.

Sergeant Briggs made his way past Lily and into the room. "Looks like I interrupted something, huh? But we can't waste any time opening presents right now."

"Oh these . . . They aren't anything important," Locke said." He put the boxes on the desk behind him and positioned himself in front of them. "Well let's get going. We don't want to keep the director waiting."

Everyone nodded in agreement.

"Now that's the Tessera spirit! You kids are going to make great soldiers someday." Kyle's voice was full of a father's pride.

As they all marched out the door, Leo breathed a sigh of relief and subtly picked up the fallen letter and pushed it into his pocket.

Upon reaching their destination, the trio said their goodbyes to the sergeant. Leo was glad that they were finally parting ways. Lily and Sergeant Briggs, on the other hand, seemed quite sad. For the entirety of their walk over, the two had been gabbing nonstop. Most of their talk was a little too technical for Leo's tastes, but those around them could easily have mistaken them for a loving father and daughter.

"If you ever need anything, Lily, don't be a stranger, you hear?" Sergeant Briggs said, with a lonesome expression on his face as he continued down the hallway. Lily gave him a big smile as she waved in reply. She then turned to the door before them and Leo knocked.

They were quickly granted entry and stood in a perfectly straight line before the directors desk.

"Thank you for coming so promptly. What I have to tell you is extremely urgent and also highly classified. I hope you understand the gravity of my meaning. Well, to put it bluntly, there was an attack. I won't go into the specifics, but it seems beyond a shadow of a doubt that we have at least one spy in our facility. After the, um, attack, the colonel was able to discover some evidence of the saboteurs' identities."

Leo hung on every word as the director paused and pulled something out from his desk. Although it didn't show on their faces, Leo assumed the others, like him, were beginning to break out in a cold sweat. Lily and Locke had left a bag full of evidence behind but only as a red herring to try and fool their pursuers. Watching the director closely, he could only pray that their trick had worked.

"This is what he found . . . It belongs to you? Yes?"

What the director had placed on the table before them was something that they were all familiar with and had all seen the day of the Founding Celebration. Locke's face instantly went pale at the sight, and for good reason. He was the last person to have officially used said evidence on the table.

"It was found the other day, poorly hidden in the mess hall. We believe that the person or persons who were the last to use this were the culprits of not only the incident there but also of the larger attack last night."

The director studied the three as he held the remote controller closer to them.

"You look like you're about to be sick, Locke. Do you have anything you wish to tell me now?"

Even though he was innocent of the incident in question, Locke said nothing. Leo wondered what the fake evidence was that Lily and Locke had planted and who it implicated. Also, he was almost positive that the remote hadn't been a part of the fake evidence, since Locke had lost it when Sarah was not present.

Unless Sarah did have other accomplices, as she had implied. It was very possible that she had set them up. Locke had to be under a lot of mental stress. For someone like him, who was pretty adept at handling such things, to have it show on his face really put into perspective how volatile their situation was.

"It . . . It's just . . . I was the last person to use it before the celebration," Locke finally said. "I was in charge of using the robot to move all the food and tables into position. But after we began eating, due to my carelessness I . . . I somehow lost it. I was so afraid when I realized it was gone . . . and then everything happened. I didn't know what to think or what to do. I was terrified that it was all my fau—"

The director held up his hand, stopping Locke midconfession. "It's all right, my boy, I was just testing you. I wanted to see if you would tell me the truth or not. I'm glad that you did. Trust is something I value above all else. In truth we've already figured out what happened and how the remote was stolen from your possession.

"You see, when we recovered the evidence, we had scanned it for fingerprints and DNA. The test results showed there were only two people that had recently handled the remote. One was you and the other was," the director reached back into his desk, "the young man in this photo right here." He placed a picture before them. "You know him, don't you?"

To Leo's utter shock, he recognized the person being shown to them. They all knew him.

"I can't believe it, but it makes sense now," Locke said. "That's why he was trying to be so annoying and get close to me while we were eating. He wanted to get close and distract me, to pickpocket the remote without me noticing."

"You're right, Locke," Leo said. "He did seem really strange that whole day. He is normally so serious and strict, but that entire day he was making jokes and acting totally out of character." Leo didn't know if he believed what the director had shown them yet, but he at least wanted to help bolster Locke's credibility in front of the director.

"What you have just told me matches up with the intel I have received," said the director. "We already did some digging, nothing to draw attention to him yet, just to get a feel for how he was acting the day of the incident. It seems as though he was acting very unlike himself that day. So, with my information, and cross checking it with what you have just told me, I have decided to give you three your first mission."

"Sooo, you want us to spy on Luke, right?" Lily instantly clapped her hands over her mouth. She had spoken out loud and out of turn, but it seemed that the director had not minded in the slightest.

"To put it plainly, yes. Due to your recent position as students, being constantly around and familiar with the suspected individual, it seems perfect for you three to investigate him without drawing unnecessary attention. If he is truly a spy and not just some false lead, we would not want him to realize he is being surveilled by us.

"You will begin to track all his movements and monitor his interactions, no matter how small, from this moment on until further notice. I would like detailed reports daily, and if anything of significance happens, I would like you to use the items I gave you the other day to contact me directly, and then I will send someone directly to you."

Leo and Locke nodded their heads in agreement, while it seemed Lily was slightly confused. Although she did not say anything, it was obvious to Leo that she didn't realize the director was referring to the gift they still had not opened. It appeared that it was some type of device for direct communication with the director.

It seemed the director was planning for such a situation. Leo couldn't help but admire the man's forethought and preparation. Even though the man before them could now be considered an enemy and a threat to their survival, Leo still couldn't help but feel somewhat comforted by how thorough and capable the director truly was.

On the other hand, Leo had an ominous feeling that things were going too well, and a small part of him was screaming that the director somehow knew of their involvement, and that it was all just a trap.

"If irrefutable evidence is found, we must act swiftly to capture and interrogate him. We cannot have him signal any other possible spies that may be lurking within my facility. I am aware that he is your friend and classmate, but if it comes to it, you may even need to dispose of him with your own hands. However unlikely, I just want you to be prepared if that situation ever arises. I have high hopes for you three . . . Do not disappoint me."

"Yes sir! Do not worry about us," Locke said. "We will find out the truth. If Luke really is a spy, his life is forfeit. We will do what needs to be done to protect our home and the only hope for the world."

Even the director was taken aback by this display of passion, but eventually broke into a large smile.

"Good to hear! I wish I had an entire army of good men like you. If that were the case, we could save the world that much faster. Well, good luck and remember . . . We are always watching." The director gave them a crisp salute and dismissed them with a small wave.

After returning to the safety of the hallway, Leo finally released his clenched fist. Although he hid it well, his blood was boiling the entire time the director had been speaking. He felt a calming hand on his shoulder, and Locke's sympathetic voice reached his ear.

"I'm just as angry as you are; I'm just better at hiding it. We need to do this. I don't actually believe that Luke is guilty, but we need to see him before anything else happens. We might even need to tell him what we know if it comes down to it. But first I think we need to see Sarah and confirm if Luke is one of her collaborators or not."

Leo managed to take a calming breath. Lily said, "I really don't think Luke could be doing anything bad. He never struck me as that type of person. What I've been thinking about though, was what the director said. I wonder what kind of devices he gave us? I bet it's super-advanced communication tech or something."

Of course, that's what was on her mind. Leo's anger subsided, and he smiled wearily as they continued down the hall.

The corridors were much more crowded now than they were before, and they made slow but steady progress towards Sarah's apartment. They had hoped to catch her before she left to teach her first class, but at the rate that they were going Leo did not know if they would be able to make it in time.

Finally reaching the familiar doorway, they knocked, but it seemed that they had already missed her. Just to make sure, they tried to knock several times and even tried to open it, but with no success.

Leo turned to his companions. "She won't be back until after all her classes are over. We can't just wait around till then, especially with the director wanting daily reports. Plus, I am not breaking into her room again after what happened last time."

"True, that is how we got wrapped up in all this in the first place." Lily shrugged. "Can't we just fake the reports?"

"I wouldn't want to take that chance unless we really had to," Locke said. "I wouldn't be surprised if the director put a tail on us to make sure what we report is accurate. That's what I would do, especially with untrained, unproven people such as us."

"He does have a point, Lily," Leo said. "We need to assume we are being watched. So, what should we do?"

Suddenly, Leo's stomach let out a embarrassingly loud growl. Lily snickered. "Well I think that settles that doesn't it?? It's been forever since we've eaten anything. We can't think on an empty stomach after all, so let's go get breakfast, and then we can make our next plan."

She was right. Leo couldn't even remember the last time they had a proper meal. When a rather loud sound emanated from Locke's midsection, Lily couldn't help but crack up more at the synchronicity of their stomachs' responses. In the middle of her fit of laughter her own stomach grumbled to life. They all burst into laughter, and Leo felt his mood lighten.

They quickened their pace as they approached one of the many smaller cafeterias closest to their own living quarters. The smell of food was growing intoxicating as they stepped inside and entered the long line to wait for food.

"Ahhhh, it all smells so good! I know exactly what I'm gonna get," Lily said. That was all Leo could hear before she began to speak so excitedly that all the words seemed to blur together. Leo and Locke just nodded when it seemed appropriate. Neither had the energy to even attempt to calm her down.

Turning away from Lily, Leo noticed Luke making a beeline for them.

"I have been looking for you guys everywhere!" he said, sounding panicked, his hands a blur.

Leo could only hold up both his hands in an attempt to block the tirade of words spilling from Luke's mouth. "Whoa, slow it down . . . What's the matter Luke?"

Luke continued to spew an incoherent jumble of words, with his arms frantically flailing about in every direction. Nothing Leo nor Locke could do would get him under control. Lily finally shoved a biscuit that she had pulled off some poor passerby's tray straight into Luke's open mouth, managing to get him under control.

Leo could not tell whether to feel lucky that their mission just so happened to find them so soon or unlucky that they hadn't had a chance to confirm his status with Sarah. Either way, this could be a difficult situation.

Locke began to ask Luke some basic questions as he struggled to swallow the food.

"You said you were looking for us? Why? What's going on?"

"Well, I-I-I've been hearing things . . . Rumors about you guys a-and I think you might be able to help me."

Luke looked around as he spoke. Thankfully it seemed that he was being purposely vague with all the people around

"What rumors are you talking about?" Locke said. "You sound like you're in some sort of trouble or something."

Luke kept silent for a moment as he anxiously fidgeted with his hands. Then seeming to come to a decision, he uncharacteristically lowered his head and spoke in a low, trembling voice. "Please . . . I don't know what to do . . . I don't know who to turn to besides you three."

Luke's apparent fear did not sway Locke in the slightest. "Tell us what happened. From the way you're sounding . . . What did you do?"

Luke did not respond to any of Locke's questions as he continued to look towards his feet.

Lily punched Locke in the arm. "Don't be mean to Luke! He came to us for help. We should at least hear him out before you bury him in intimidating questions."

Locke turned to the pouting Lily and rubbed the spot where she had punched him. "You didn't have to hit me though . . . That actually hurt!"

Leo ignored the two bickering beside him and put a hand on Luke's shoulder. "Ignore those two. If we can, we would be happy to help you. But in order to do that, we really do need to know what it is you are so worried about."

Luke slowly looked up at Leo and nodded his head.

Leo said, "All right then, let's get out of here. We should go somewhere more private. Let's head back to my room."

He turned and separated the still bickering Lily and Locke, forcefully grabbing them by their arms, and dragged them out of the cafeteria, with Luke following at their heels.

Leo continued to drag them like misbehaving children the entire way, ignoring their embarrassed protests. Finally releasing them from his grasp as he opened the door to his room, he herded the three inside. Before following them inside, he took a look around. It seemed no one had followed them, but he couldn't shake the feeling that they were still being watched.

Leo took one last look around, then he stepped inside and closed the door. He motioned to Luke to sit in the sole chair in the room, and he and the others sat on the bed across from Luke.

"Ok, now explain everything to us. But try to remain calm, ok? The calmer you are, the better you can explain what's going on, and only then, maybe, we will be able to help you."

Luke rested his elbows on his knees and leaned forward as he took a deep breath. "I might have done something really, really bad . . . I didn't mean for it to happen, but it . . . it just kinda happened. I-I'm so stupid."

Placing his head in his hands, it appeared that Luke was on the verge of tears. "I didn't steal it, I swear! I just found it laying there. It just got so out of hand so fast . . . I didn't know what to do!" Luke seemed to be on the verge of another breakdown.

"Ok, ok," Leo said. "Whatever it was, it wasn't your fault. It . . . it was just an accident, right? But what was it you found?"

Luke looked up when he heard the word "accident" and looked off into the distance for a moment.

"Accident? No, your right . . . It was all just an accident. The remote . . . It just went crazy . . . short circuited or something. It couldn't have been my fault. It was just an accident . . ."

Leo's, Lily's, and Locke's eyes all went wide. They of course all knew of Luke's possible connection with the remote and his possibility of being a spy. But after listening to Luke and watching his seemingly genuine, fear-filled reaction, Leo felt Luke was truly innocent of being a spy, which just led to more questions about what he had done and why he even had the remote in the first place.

Locke spoke up. His question was blunt, but he had a very important reason for asking it. It would be to definitively find out what Luke's true intentions were, completely innocent or otherwise.

"So, what were you doing with the remote if it wasn't your fault, then? We know that they only recovered two sets of fingerprints on it, mine and yours."

For the first time since entering the room Luke's eyes met with Locke's. They were filled with terror.

"I-I was right . . . They sent you three to watch me, didn't they?"

Locke solemnly nodded. "Yes, we were given orders to keep an eye on you and report all that we found out back to the director. They believe you are a spy or are, at least, associated with spies hiding within the facility."

"You-you don't believe them . . . Do you??? I promise you I didn't mean for anything like that to happen. I swear!"

"I want to believe you, but it does seem rather suspicious. For us to believe you, you need to come clean about everything. The more you hide, the worse you will look later."

Luke sighed as his gaze returned to examining his feet. "It was like I said. I didn't steal the remote. I found it. I swear. After you three were called up to the stage, I saw it lying under the table where you were sitting, so I picked it up.

"At the time, I knew that Locke had been using it earlier, and I was angry with you . . . Locke. You were not being very nice to me, and I wanted to get back at you somehow. So, I hatched a plan to take the remote. Then after you realized you lost it, I would offer to give it back to you . . . But only after you got in trouble for losing it.

"But when I picked it up, it somehow activated. The robot went out of control, and I tried to stop it. I didn't know how to use it and ended up making it all worse. I got so scared, after everyone's reactions, especially the colonel's. I thought it would be best if I kept quiet, so I hid the remote in the dining hall. Ever since then I have been scared for my life. Everyone's been on the lookout for spies, and I have been so afraid that they will find and kill me for being a traitor . . . even though I'm not."

Locke turned and prodded Lily in the arm. "See! I told you that thing was hard to control."

As Lily and Locke began another squabble, Leo sighed and turned back to the increasingly terrified Luke.

"I understand why you are so scared. It's true that we were given orders by the director to spy on you. Luckily, we are no allies of the director or the colonel, so don't worry. I believe you. You are innocent. However, I don't think that the higher-ups will view it that way. Even if you came clean to them, I still think you would be punished, maybe even be made an example of to show the others the consequences of disrespecting leadership and, more importantly, to make a statement aimed at the traitors that they know are within the facility."

"You-you-you think they would kill me??? Just to scare the spies and make them run away?"

"To be honest," Locke said, "they would probably do much worse than just kill you to make an example. If it was me—"

Lily covered his mouth with her hand. "Stop it Locke!"

"He does not need to hear the details," Leo said. "I think he can imagine that for himself."

During the long, awkward silence that followed, an idea popped into Leo's head. He had no idea if it was a good one, but it didn't seem like it would be any worse than their current situation. "Luke, could you go into the hall for a minute? I would really appreciate it. I have to ask Lily and Locke something private. I'll call you back in when we are done."

"Uh . . . ok. I'll go wait right outside then."

Luke slowly stood up and walked out the door. He seemed to understand that Leo planned to discuss the pros and cons of helping him without trying to directly hurt his feelings.

As the door shut, Locke crossed his arms and narrowed his eyes. "You want to tell him about our situation, don't you? I think that is a bad idea. He might go off and try to rat us out to save his own skin."

Lily's expression was the exact opposite of Locke's. "Well, I think it's a good idea," she said. "He doesn't seem like the type to sell us out, especially since he already knew we were supposed to spy on him. Coming clean to us tells me that he can be trusted."

"Locke, I know it's a risk," Leo said. "But I don't want to tell him about everything just yet, just the general situation. Then maybe later on we can fill him in on everything. As of now I just think it would be in our best interest to gain as many hands and minds as we can. Especially if he really doesn't know anything about Sarah. Then we can use him to help us behind the scenes, if we can get him cleared by the director, that is."

Locke raised his hands in defeat. "Fine, fine. Do whatever you think is right. I might not trust Luke, but I trust your judgment.

But I'm still going to keep my eyes on him . . . Now Lily, can you please stop hitting me!?!"

"Only if you promise to try to be nice. If he joins us, we need to make him feel at least a little welcome."

Lily finally stopped jabbing at Locke's side and bounded over to the door to call Luke back in. Leo exchanged a quick glance with Locke, wondering if he was also thinking it odd that Lily was being so open and friendly with people other than them lately, first with Sergeant Briggs and now with Luke. It seemed that all these recent events were beginning to change her. Leo looked down at his own hands. He didn't feel any different. Maybe he just wasn't aware of his own changes quite yet.

With Luke back in the room, Leo began their story from the top, planning to leave out any names or specific locations that could be used against them.

"Well, all this started when you just so happened to wreck the celebration the other day. You see, we have what we like to call our secret base somewhere in the facility. Lily likes to think of it as her workshop. She keeps many of her plans and projects stored there. She was so upset by the possibility of one of her creations going out of control that she ran away to check her schematics for the robot.

"While we were looking for her, the three of us overheard the director, the colonel, and a bunch of others talking about the possibility of spies in the facility and, how should I put this . . . other sensitive information about the three of us.

"We then decided to go speak to the director and tell him what we knew about the incident in the dining hall to try to clear things up. While we were there, he ended up recruiting us and gave us a mission to look for any possible spies behind the scenes.

We couldn't really refuse, and it just so happens that we ended up finding the real spy shortly afterward.

"I don't think you would believe me even if I told you who it is, so right now we'll keep that confidential for our own protection. After we found out about this person, I ended up getting taken hostage at gunpoint. We were then forced to become her accomplices under threat of death. So, I completely understand your fear about being caught. The four of us here just so happen to all be in the same boat. I believe we can help each other out, and I know we can make it out of this terrible situation alive if we work together."

Luke was on the edge of his chair the entire time Leo was catching him up to speed. To Leo's shock, however, Luke didn't seem the least surprised by what he had just been told. It almost seemed that he was excited.

"I knew it!" Luke said. "I knew something like that must have happened. I overheard some of the soldiers earlier, and they were talking about an attack that happened on the forty-seventh floor. That must have been you guys! I also saw that soldier come to your room earlier today and take you somewhere. Aaand . . . I might have followed you guys when you went to Ms. Meli's room. I bet she's the spy you found, right? Judging by your reactions, I must be right. I can't believe I was right! I'm so happy I came to see you guys after all."

"Wait!" Locke said. "You were already spying on us?"

Luke squirmed in his chair. "Uh . . . Maybe . . . Just a little bit. But it wasn't for any bad reason. I just wanted to talk to you guys. I was really scared, so I was waiting for the perfect time. But the longer I watched you guys, the more questions I had . . ."

"Fine, fine, fine; we get it," Leo said, annoyed but more than slightly impressed by Luke. Leo had been trying to remain vigilant for anyone watching them, but he hadn't even noticed Luke at all. Maybe he could be useful to them.

Leo sighed at his carefully worded story being thrown out the window. "I guess you know pretty much everything at this point. Are you sure you aren't a real spy? Because it turns out you're pretty good at it so far."

Luke raised his hands defensively. "No-no, I swear . . . I kind of just have a talent for being ignorable, so it makes it easier for me to sneak around and listen in on people."

"Well, we might need to make use of your newfound talent," Leo said, "but as of now, remember . . . we are supposed to be watching you and gathering intel. So, try to keep your distance from us, and please try not to do anything suspicious. We'll contact you if and when we need to tell you something. If an emergency happens and we need to meet in person, we'll tell you the location of our base. In case of any unforeseen events we will meet there."

Luke nodded his head vigorously. "I understand. You can rely on me. We're in this together now, after all."

Leo stood up, prompting the others to stand up as well. On their way to the door, Lily blurted out, "We should come up with a cool team name! I was thinking we could call ourselves, 'the Forty-Seven Shadows.'"

Now that was more like the Lily that Leo knew. She always loved to name everything, no matter how trivial.

Locke snickered. "Why would we use forty-seven in the name? We are only four people, after all."

"Well, it's because we were the first people to break into the forty-seventh floor, aaand it's to make it seem like we have more members! The four shadows just seem too small to me. Forty-seven seems much more intimidating."

She did have a point, Leo thought. In all honesty, he didn't really care if they had a self-appointed name or not, but he knew it would make Lily happy, so he decided to go along with it. "Let her have this one, Locke. It really isn't that bad of a name."

With the pressure of both Leo and Luke, Locke quickly caved and accepted the name. They finally waved their good-byes to Luke and returned inside.

Lily was the first inside and dove face first onto the bed. However, her swan dive was so forceful it bumped the bed into the desk, knocking its contents all over the floor.

Chastising Lily's childish behavior, Locke finally noticed the unopened boxes, now on the floor, that the director had given to them. With his curiosity now piqued, he quickly opened the first box, with Leo watching from over his shoulder.

The moment Locke saw the contents, the box almost slipped through his fingers. Leo felt his chest tighten. In the box was a set of three communication earpieces and their respective receivers. They were just like those they saw the soldiers often wear, which in itself was not very alarming, but a red light was flashing on one of the receivers. It had been turned on.

Lily looked inquisitively up at them from her position on the bed. "Hey! What was in the box??? You both look like you've seen a ghost or something."

She jumped up and snatched the box from Locke's loose grip. "Oh this . . . I guess you guys thought it was on or something right? Ha, nope. Don't worry guys. This just means it needs to be charged, that's all."

Hearing her casual explanation, a sudden wave of relief

washed over Leo. Locke broke into a nervous smile. In a matter of moments, they had gone from total fear to hugely relieved.

"Thank God!" Locke said, in a voice still slightly trembling. "We just dodged a bullet. Imagine us confessing to all those things if there had been a listening device right next to us the whole time. From now on no more talking about anything incriminating out loud. We can't risk it."

Leo couldn't have agreed more. As he turned to Lily, he saw she had not been listening to Locke at all, and her face had turned stark white.

"Lily . . . What's—"

"Oh no..." she said and dropped the second box. With the contents still within her grasp, she made a silent beeline for the door and fled the room.

Chasing her into the hallway, Leo called out to her for some sort of explanation. However, Lily was lost in her own world, and the only response that Leo could get was "Wait in the room and get things ready to escape."

Returning to his room, Leo was greeted by the sight of Locke looking quite nervous, sitting on the edge of the bed. "Where is she? Weren't you following her?"

Leo slowly shook his head. "I was . . . but she managed to give me the slip. It was almost like she was possessed or something. She's never been able to outrun me before."

"But did you manage to get anything out of her before you lost her?"

"She said, and I quote, 'Wait in the room and get things ready to escape.' I honestly don't know if I heard her correctly, but it sounds like whatever was in the box got her scared enough to think we need to be ready to move."

Locke smacked his forehead with the palm of his hand. "Why, of all times, would she just run out of here now and not tell us anything. If we really need to escape now, wouldn't the best course of action be to stay together?"

Leo also could not fathom why she had run away all of a sudden, but he couldn't ignore it. "Well, we should listen to her for now. Let's quickly pack our necessities together and then meet back up with her. I'm almost positive she went back to the hideout. That's the direction she was headed. It makes the most sense."

Locke nodded and, without any words, began piling up all the things that they would need to take with them if they were to try to escape the facility.

They placed their meager belongings within three backpacks and quickly exited the room. Leo tried his best to make sure that no one was watching them as they made their way to their hideout and, hopefully, to Lily, as well.

10

LOYALTY

AS SOON AS LEO and Locke finally made it back inside their base, they threw down everything they were carrying and collapsed to the floor in exhaustion.

As they caught their breath, they first heard then saw Rusty bounding around one of the many towers of boxes. Leo could tell by the mechanical canine's reaction that Lily was indeed here, just as he had suspected.

Leo was so tired from hauling the overstuffed packs, that he couldn't even muster the strength to defend himself against the assaulting Rusty.

"Good boy . . . good boy. Could you get Lily for us please? We are so tired."

Rusty tilted his head for a moment as his tongue temporarily stopped its attack on Leo's face. He seemed to be processing whether or not he would do as he was asked.

It wasn't until Locke joined in, with his inclusion of a small bribe of fresh oil, that Rusty finally turned and ran down one of the many pathways through the boxes. Leo and Locke just hoped it was in the direction of Lily, as they both struggled to sit up right.

Quite a few minutes passed with no sign of either Rusty or Lily. Finally, having regained some of their lost stamina, Leo and Locke decided they couldn't wait any longer, and they carefully made their way towards the far side of the room.

What greeted them was an empty workbench and an even emptier room beyond it. Neither Lily nor Rusty could be found anywhere even though traces of Lily's work were freshly scattered about.

"She must be looking through some of the boxes for something. She couldn't have gone far," Leo said as he approached the workbench.

It appeared that she had been in a hurry to examine something very tiny. All the items that had once been on the table were now strewn across the ground, replaced by a microscope and some instruments meant for handling tiny electrical devices placed dead center on the table before them.

Leo was getting a bad feeling as he carefully looked at the tools scattered about the table. Normally Lily was very methodical when it came to her tools. She must have been in a panic.

"We should double back and see if we can find her, maybe she was buried alive under one of the towers of boxes . . ."

Locke scoffed at the idea, but also nodded at Leo's half-hearted attempt at a joke. They looked down each row of boxes as they moved back towards the entrance. It was only when they reached the last few rows that the mechanical tapping of Rusty and the soft footfalls of Lily became audible.

As they rounded the corner, Lily, who appeared to be deep in thought, jumped from surprise. "Oh! It's just you guys . . . How long have you been here? I told Leo to wait in the room and get things ready for us to leave!"

It was obvious from her frantic tone that she was scared. "What are you up to over here?" Locke said. "We were just looking all over for you, and we didn't see you over here before. Did you leave and just come back?"

Locke was being forward with his questions as per usual, but Lily's nervous demeanor somehow seemed unnatural, even for her.

"Noooo, I have been here the entire time! I was just looking for something I needed in one of these boxes. You probably just didn't see me because I was in between the rows. These boxes are really big, after all."

Locke did not seem satisfied with her answer in the slightest. Leo cut him off.

"Locke, I know what you're thinking, but we don't have the time for twenty questions right now. If she said she was here the whole time, then she was. But Lily, you really need to tell us what this is all about. What did you find?"

Without a word, Lily reached out and grabbed the two by their hands and led them back towards her workbench. Once there she set three small items on the table.

"These are not what they appear to be . . . What do they look like to you two?"

"I don't know," Leo said. "Aren't those just the special ribbons they give out to students who graduate from the academy?"

Lily shook her head as she pointed her finger towards the top part of the ribbon. "That is only what they appear to be. Inside of the metal part of the ribbon, at the top where you clasp it to your clothes, I found a radio microtransmitter."

She moved her finger along the length of the ribbon and

stopped at the end. "And at this end I also found an extremely tiny microphone."

Leo was shocked. Why would they be given a hidden communication device if they had already received three sets of communicators?

"How did you realize what they really were?" Locke said. "I don't think Leo or I would have ever noticed."

Lily puffed out her chest. "Of course I would notice them!" she said, her voice full of pride. "I was the one who designed the prototype for these micro listening devices. Whoever gave them to us obviously didn't know I was the one responsible for their initial development."

Leo and Locke were both stunned into silence. Leo had no idea that she had designed such a thing. It was a pure stroke of luck that whoever had planted the listening devices had not known about their history.

"I realized what they were as soon as I saw them, but I had no idea whether or not they were currently active or not. That's why I came rushing here as fast as possible." Lily's prideful voice had begun to crack.

"So, you came here, and judging by your reaction they must have been active, huh?" Leo said.

Lily could only slowly nod as the full weight of the situation began to set in.

"We need to leave this place now," Locke said. "We can't wait any longer. I say we gather up all the equipment we brought and leave as soon as we can. If we do it tonight, it would be our best chance at making it out."

Leo couldn't argue with Locke's plan. The listening devices must have heard everything they had told Luke, and there was no getting out of that. They had admitted to betraying Tessera with their own mouths.

They only had two options. Either stay and eventually be captured and tortured for information then executed or try their best to escape and either be killed in the attempt or live to reach the outside world. Their choice was obvious.

"We all agree that fleeing is our best option, correct?" Leo said. "But I was just thinking . . . Should we try to bring Luke with us?"

As Leo had already surmised, one of the two was for it, while the other was strongly against it. Thankfully, they came to a compromise. They would go ask Luke if he would be willing to flee with them that night or risk staying behind within the facility.

Leo knew that the coming night would be the most difficult of their lives. No one had successfully escaped the facility in over fifty years and had lived to talk about it.

With all three of their bags full to the brim, Leo, Lily, and even Locke shared a tight, threefold embrace. However, it was only Lily's eyes that flowed with fresh tears as she struggled to form her thoughts into words.

"I-I just want to say this; n-no matter what happens, you two are my family. The only family I would ever want or need. Whether it's against Tessera or even the entire world, I know if it's the three of us together, we will survive."

Locked within their embrace, Leo could not shake the feeling of foreshadowing in Lily's touching words. He hoped that it wouldn't end up coming to that point. Tessera would be enough to handle, let alone the entire world.

"Here's to seeing the outside world for the first time," Locke said. "Maybe I'll get to see the place the textbooks call the 'ocean'."

Together they made their way back through the vents and out into the closet that housed the secret entrance.

Leo was noticeably tired having just dragged himself and a full pack throughout the cramped vents for the second time. Nonetheless, since he was the first to drop down into the small closet entrance, his senses had to be on high alert.

Leo did not know why, but his animalistic instincts were going off as he watched Locke and then Lily finally drop down into the space behind him. Even though he didn't hear anything besides the normal traffic outside the door, he felt as though they were somehow being hunted. There was tension in the air, but at the moment he couldn't identify the source.

Leo tried to shake the feeling off as they prepared to find an opening and quickly leave the small supply closet.

After waiting a few moments, the sounds of movement began to quiet. Right before the trio slipped out into the hallway, Leo looked back at Lily and Locke, who had lined up behind him. Leo could tell that something was on Lily's mind. Unlike Locke, she appeared to be deep in contemplation over something. Nudging her, it took a moment before she snapped back to reality, nodding in the affirmative.

Giving Lily a reassuring smile, Leo opened the door and stepped into the hallway, followed by Locke and then Lily in turn. Surprisingly, there wasn't a single soul in sight.

Instead of lucky, Leo thought it strange. Normally at this time of day there would be at least a few people making their way through this area, but it was mysteriously empty.

As the trio rounded the hallway's first corner, Leo felt what could only be described as an electrical shock surge through-out his entire body. It radiated from the middle of his back and spread along his spine to the top of his head and down his legs to the tips of his toes. The pain was so sudden and unbearable he instantly dropped to his knees and then to the floor. The pain was so great his brain could not even register the fact that his face had smashed directly into the hallway floor, and that his nose had begun to gush blood.

Leo tried his best to fight off the blackness that was slowly starting to obscure his vision. Using the last of his will power and strength, he finally managed to move his head. Even in his current condition he had to make sure Lily and Locke were all right. The sight that greeted him, however, could not have been real. In his half-conscious state he must have been seeing things . . . He had to be seeing things . . .

Two people stood over the unmoving body of Locke. The taller figure appeared to be the figure of Colonel Veers, while the sight of the other overwhelmed Leo's fading consciousness. Standing beside the colonel and clutching a small device in her hand was Lily, an unfamiliar expression on her face.

The more Leo attempted to struggle against the darkness, the faster it dragged him under. The last things his conscious mind formed before he finally slipped into the depths of unconsciousness were three simple words. *Was she smiling?*

• • •

Leo's eyes flickered as he began to stir. He hovered somewhere between being fully asleep and fully awake.

Trying to shake his brain fog, he thought about the strange dream he had just been having. Something about having to flee his home, that his and his friends' lives had been in danger . . . And something else that Leo just couldn't put his finger on . . . A face . . . An expression . . . A smile?

Leo struggled to remember what it had been about. He knew deep down that something important must have happened in it, something he needed to remember . . . But now it was as if he was trying to grasp at smoke floating in the wind.

Beginning to wake up, he let out a large yawn as he tried to wipe the sleepiness from his eyes, but mysteriously neither of his arms responded. Lily and Locke must have snuck into his bed without his knowledge again . . .

Finally gaining the energy, he managed to open his eyes, and when his vision finally came back into focus, the sight that greeted him was anything but familiar.

The bare walls of the tiny room that surrounded him were hypnotically white, without any trace of blemish or imperfection. The only word to describe the strange room would be sterile. There was nothing else in the room besides Leo, who, upon looking down at himself, realized to his horror why he was unable to touch his face.

Within the pristinely white room, Leo was strapped to what appeared to be a medical gurney. Both his legs and arms were locked down without the slightest room for movement. Frantically trying to get an idea of where he was, the memories of how he had gotten here flooded back to him like an ocean wave crashing upon the shore.

They had been ambushed by the colonel and taken captive as they were leaving the entrance to their base. Were Locke and Lily all right?

Leo instinctively looked around again and called out into the empty room just to be 100 percent sure that his eyes were not playing tricks on him, and they weren't somewhere nearby.

"Lily!!! . . . Locke!!! Are you there?! Can you hear me?"

To Leo's dismay, no one replied to his call. Straining to hear anything, the only sound that greeted him was the rhythmic thumping of his own beating heart.

Trapped within the empty room, the only thing Leo could do was to think. He had no idea of how long he had been there. A few minutes? A few hours?

As each second passed, Leo couldn't help but think about the condition of Lily and Locke. He could only assume that they were both stuck in a situation similar to his own.

However, no matter what he thought about, one thing constantly kept circling back in his mind, the very last memory he had before he blacked out. In his half-conscious state he had thought he had seen the vague image of Lily standing together with the colonel.

The longer he thought about it, the more he tried to rationalize that he had either imagined it or had misunderstood what had truly happened. Leo tried his best to force his nagging thoughts down, but the more he tried to forget, the stronger they returned.

She must have been trying to fight him off or something. Or maybe she was just so shocked at what had happened she froze up. Leo tried everything he could to convince himself that the events he remembered were false, but one key detail kept crawling back.

No matter how many times he tried to remember the events in his head, Leo just couldn't forget that smile he saw. It was one he had never seen her make before. It looked almost as though someone had put on a mask of Lily, her smooth features twisted and distorted.

Leo convinced himself that what he had seen was just a product of his delirious state. However, that single image still haunted his thoughts. He became sick of being stuck within his own mind and, as he slowly became more desperate, he came up with a haphazardly crafted plan.

One singular goal drove Leo on, to make sure his friends were still alive. How he reached that goal was of little consequence. His arms and legs were pinned down, but he could still slightly rock his body from side to side within the confines of the gurney. Leo's plan was to rock his body enough to try to flip the gurney on its side, in an attempt to either become free or draw the attention of someone outside.

When the gurney hit the floor, Leo momentarily regretted his decision. He quickly overcame the pain and focused his mind on his bindings. After flipping the gurney, the frame had seemed to weaken, and Leo could feel that the straps that were holding him in place had started to loosen ever so slightly.

He continued to try wiggling both his arms and his legs. After a few minutes of near constant struggling, Leo paused to catch his breath. He could feel that his left leg was close to becoming free, but sadly both his arms had made little progress.

Leo couldn't help but to become frustrated at his current situation. His constant struggling had caused the skin on both his wrists and ankles to become raw, and the awkwardness of being on his side, mixed with the pain from his restraints, had started to take its toll on Leo's mental state.

"Aaaah! Why did this have to happen to us! Lily! Locke! Where are you?!"

All he could do was scream helplessly into the empty room until his voice eventually gave out. Mentally and physically exhausted, he closed his eyes. Even though he was stuck in such an uncomfortable position, he could feel himself beginning to doze off.

Moments before he fell asleep, he heard multiple footsteps approaching from outside and became fully awake. The door to the room opened, and though Leo had mentally prepared himself for what might befall him, his blood turned cold.

Colonel Heinrich Veers stood before him in the immaculate uniform of the highest-ranking military officer within Tessera's eastern facility. Flanking him were a man in a surgical mask and an armed soldier.

"Well now . . . It looks like we caught you in a most compromising position, haven't we?" A sinister smile crossed his normally stern face.

"It seems that my intuition was correct after all. I'm glad that I planted those listening devices within those 'gifts.' I sincerely must thank you . . . or to be more precise, I should thank your little friend. She has been a great help to me and my work. It does get tiresome always hunting for spies, after all. I much prefer the end result of the hunt for traitors. I love to see my prey after they have been cornered, with nowhere left to turn. It is a very different experience capturing traitors instead of soldiers. They usually have a similar expression to the one that is currently on your face, albeit with some subtle differences.

"For example, let's say that today I captured an enemy soldier whose allies were annihilated after a devastating battle. The look he might give me could be one full of sadness, regret, and anger. Sadness for the loss of his comrades. Regret for either his own or comrades' shortcomings during the battle. Anger towards me, the enemy that took all he held dear away. But your face, the face of a traitor, does not reflect such honorable traits.

"Your expression is full of weakness. You are sad but only have yourself to blame. You are full of regret, not for your actions but for the actions of others. You are not angry with your mortal enemies but only with yourself. Your face is full of dishonor . . . You are no soldier. You are nothing but a weakling and a coward."

The colonel spat on Leo and turned to the men at his side.

"Look, gentlemen, for this is the face of a coward, a spy, and, worst of all, a traitor. Tessera has given him everything, and this is how he repays us. He and his traitorous companion collaborated with the enemy to sabotage our future victory. I will not let this affront to Tessera stand."

After acknowledgment from his lackeys, the colonel returned his gaze to Leo. However, the entirety of the time the colonel had been talking, Leo had not listened at all. All he could think about was one thing, and before the colonel could open his mouth to continue, Leo let loose his anger, and his words echoed off the walls in the empty room.

"What have you done with Lily and Locke? If you have done anything to them, I will kill you!!!"

The colonel remained steadfast, his expression unchanged in the slightest by Leo's threatening tone. "Oh, you would kill me? Son, you'll have to do better than that. I hear that threat on a daily basis. In reality, it will be me who would kill you . . . nice and slowly. However, you are one lucky boy. The director has other plans for you and your companion. Actually, I think it is as good a time as any to bring in another visitor. I think she might be able to explain what will become of you better than I ever could. I also think you might enjoy it more if she is the one to tell you what is about to happen . . ."

At the colonel's signal, another person entered the room. It was someone that Leo knew very well, but it still took Leo a few seconds to process what he was seeing. Lily took up her position next to the colonel. She now looked completely different than when she had been with Leo and Locke.

Instead of the standard navy-colored school uniform that she normally wore, she was now dressed in an all-black uniform that Leo had never seen before. While he looked on speechless, Leo could see that the colonel had reached into his pocket and withdrew what appeared to be a small knife.

With a deadly silence, the colonel approached the still restrained Leo, knife in hand and a stern expression on his face. Still in shock at the sudden sight of Lily, all Leo could do was try his best to recoil as the colonel moved the knife closer.

"Don't be so scared. I'm not going to hurt you just yet. You can be as scared and cry as much as you want later. But right now, just be good and quiet."

The colonel spoke down to Leo in a hushed tone as he slowly brought the knife dangerously close, pointing its glistening tip towards Leo's exposed throat. However, instead of slicing Leo to ribbons, with one fluid motion he removed the sewn emblem from Leo's left shoulder. It happened so fast that Leo barely understood what had just occurred.

The colonel stood up and turned to Lily. "This is for you. For all that you have done to honor Tessera by exposing these traitors, I bestow upon you this emblem."

The colonel then took the large number one that he had removed from Leo's arm and pinned it to the vacant left shoulder of Lily's new uniform. "Now you are officially the sole Pillar of

Tessera. I look forward to all the great things you will accomplish in the future."

Leo opened his mouth and tried to call out to Lily, but the words were caught in his throat. For the first time since entering the room, Lily looked down at Leo's pathetic form as she began to speak. Her face showed little emotion. If anything, the words she spoke revealed more than her face ever could.

"My thanks, Colonel Veers," she said, "for allowing me, with this honor, to take the first of many steps I need in order to achieve my goal. With this I will no longer have to live in the shadows of my so-called friends. Now my work will be fully recognized and supported. It will become the sole light for the future that Tessera seeks. With Tessera fully backing my creations, there will be no one who can stop us."

Leo was utterly confused. What did she mean by "living in their shadows"?

The colonel clapped as a twisted smile formed on his face. "Yes, my dear! You will no longer be held down by those two liars and deceivers. You and your machines are spectacular. I almost feel bad for the fools on the council who never had the foresight to see the possibilities of your inventions. But not me. I saw the technological marvels for what they truly are. With you at the spearhead instead of this traitor, we can bolster our military might several times over with the help of your designs."

Leo's mind felt as if it were being filled with water. Everything he saw and heard wasn't making any sense to him. *Has Lily betrayed us? How could she? We were like family.*

Leo couldn't come to terms with the facts that were laid out plain as day before him. He could not, no, would not accept it.

But then the memory of the smile she had made before he lost consciousness pierced through the fog of his own denial.

"Why, Lily? Why did you smile when you hurt me and Locke? Did you really hate us that much?!?"

Lily's cold eyes met Leo's. "Why??? You ask me why?!?" Her voice trembled. "You of all people should know why! You and Locke always treated me as nothing more than a child. Always looking out for me, always helping me, never treating me as an equal. You especially . . . I always resented you, for no matter what you would do, everyone always seemed to like you the most. They would always compare us to you. Even though it was plain to see that I was superior! The only reason I ever put up with the both of you was because I saw it as my only shot of advancing. I knew that if there was ever a chance to truly surpass you, I would do anything I could to exploit it.

"When everything happened and you chose to betray Tessera, I knew it was the perfect opportunity to gain the position I so rightfully deserved. After Locke and I discovered the truth of our origins, I realized I was not who I thought I was. That realization finally gave me the perspective I needed. We are nothing more than tools, and if I was to live as a tool of Tessera, I would do it only if I could achieve my true goal in the process. Thankfully, it only cost me two pathetic friends to finally be on my way to reaching my goal. I would gladly do it over again and again and again."

The longer Lily spoke, the more her voice shook with rage. Leo couldn't believe what he was hearing. Every word she spoke was like a hot knife being plunged into his heart.

"But we were a family!" he said. "We always had each other's back! You can't tell me all that was a lie." The pain in Leo's voice was obvious, and he felt as though he was about to cry.

"Ha! Such a poor little boy," the colonel said. "You learned this lesson a little too late. Only the strongest and most cunning survive in this world. However, this time it seems that you were not the fittest nor the most cunning. She, who you thought was your friend, was your undoing. Now we have wasted enough time with this trash. Lily, explain to this pathetic fool what will become of him and his friend due to his own weakness."

The colonel waved his hand as if to rush the process. "There is much work that still needs to be done after all; we still need to locate that witch of a teacher." He patted Lily's shoulder and exited the room.

The only ones remaining in the room other than Leo, were Lily and the two other men that had initially entered with the colonel. Doing as she had been instructed, Lily pulled out an official-looking sheet of paper and began reading its contents aloud.

"By order of Colonel Veers and approved by Director Anderson, the boy known as Leo, formerly number one, will henceforth have his current mind and all past memories erased. His body will be immediately transferred to Dr. Jacobs on the forty-seventh floor. It is his wish to perform experiments investigating the effects of long-term genetic manipulation and cloning. The same order is to be applied to the one named Locke, formerly designated number two."

Leo had begun to silently sob. "Tell me why!"

As Lily looked up from the paper, she did not make eye contact with Leo. She made an expression of disgust, her jaw clenched, and turned on her heel and walked straight out the door. She never turned around or made the slightest indication that she had heard his desperate pleading.

11

ATTACK AND DEFEND

SOME TIME HAD PASSED since Lily had left the room, and now Leo was again alone. He was grateful that the masked man and the soldier had at least righted his gurney before rushing to follow Lily. Free of the pain that had been plaguing him, Leo could now fully process the shocking events that had just transpired, but he had no idea what to think. What Lily told him had come completely by surprise. This entire time, for the years that they had all known each other, not once had he seen the side of Lily that he just witnessed. It seemed that she had become a different person.

Leo had seen Lily become angry before, either at himself or Locke, but this situation was utterly different. To see the irritation on her face, to hear her voice trembling with rage, was enough to shock Leo to the very core.

On top of all that, what she had said had done even more damage to Leo's psyche. He couldn't help but think that if she had been honest with them from the beginning, maybe it could have ended differently.'

In that moment, Leo's tears finally stopped and were replaced by a single, all-consuming thought. He had to know why . . . He had to find out the real reason why she had betrayed them.

Even after all that she had said, Leo wasn't satisfied with her explanation. He needed to know beyond a shadow of a doubt. He needed to talk with her alone, face to face. Only then, would he be satisfied. Only when he was convinced of her true intentions would he choose to leave her here.

Because he was leaving, Leo didn't know how just yet, but he would find Locke, and they would escape this place together.

In Leo's mind, the three would escape together and live peacefully in the outside world, far away from Tessera and from its troubles. But if he confronted Lily and it ended up that she had told him the truth, he would respect her wishes.

Even after all she had done to both Leo and Locke, he couldn't bring himself to hate her. Leo didn't know if there was something fundamentally wrong with him or not. Even though he knew most people would be furious if they were in the same situation, no matter how hard, he tried he just couldn't become angry.

It might have been possible that some of what Lily had said about him and Locke contained a fraction of the truth, but Leo just didn't want to consciously accept it.

However, none of that mattered at the moment. He dried his eyes on his shoulder. *First things first.* He needed to figure out a way of freeing himself from his restraints. Then he could plan on finding Locke, confronting Lily, and then escaping with them, together hand in hand.

"But how the hell am I going to do all that!!!" Leo screamed.

Suddenly the whole room shook. Leo was so stunned by what he thought was the force produced by his own voice, that he stopped screaming into the empty room. Startled, and beginning to think that he was going crazy again, the only thing he could think to do was to yell again into the void.

Before he could even open his mouth again, the room began to shake violently. *Earthquake.* He had experienced a few tremors in his lifetime within the facility but nothing of this magnitude.

That word quickly exited his mind and was replaced by a new word, "attack." Unlike a normal earthquake, it felt like the entire facility was being shaken by multiple large explosions.

• • •

In reality, Leo was not too far away from the truth. The shock-waves that Leo had felt were the large explosions of a certain military force's initial wave of attack, which moments before had drilled their way past the facility's first line of defense and then proceeded to blow large holes into the exterior walls of the compound. Ground troops from said organization then poured into Tessera's easternmost facility.

Although Leo didn't know it at the time, the facility was facing its largest attack since its very inception. It would also coincidentally be the perfect opportunity that Leo needed to attempt his daring escape.

As Leo began to resist the straps, the violent shaking stopped and was replaced by loud shouting from right outside, in what Leo assumed was an outer hallway.

Leo couldn't quite make out words, but he could hear loud voices, followed by low mechanical rumbles and the sounds of metal hitting metal as they passed by his doorway.

Finally catching a break, Leo managed to free one of his feet from its restraint. As he did so, the sounds from outside suddenly stopped and there were a few moments of piercing silence. Leo tried to listen closely as he worked on freeing his other leg.

A single gunshot broke the silence. What followed could only be described as deafening.

To Leo, it sounded like a full-scale war was going on right outside the room.

He had never in his life heard more than the average gunshot during his training, but this was an experience like none other. Even from the other side of the wall, Leo couldn't even imagine the carnage that was happening, as a hail of bullets pelted the metal door to his room.

The skirmish was short but intense, not lasting more than ten minutes. The entire time, all Leo could do was pray that the door would hold under the torrent of impacts.

He breathed a small sigh of relief as the sounds of the gunfire and explosions seemed to slowly move farther away. Leo assumed that this attack was a direct result of Sarah and the message she had sent. But before he could think about the purpose of the sudden attack, the battered door to his room groaned to life.

A familiar figure burst through the now opened doorway.

"Locke! Get me out of here!!!"

Leo didn't even care how Locke was standing before him. All he wanted was to be free from the gurney.

"So, that's how you greet your savior??? Not even a 'How are you here, Locke?' I see how it is . . ."

Locke couldn't help but to poke fun at Leo as he made his way cautiously over to Leo's position.

"I will say this though, those straps definitely match your style. I wouldn't be surprised if you asked me to take them along, too."

"Ha-ha. Make all the jokes you want. Just get me out of these things!"

As they continued to banter, Locke managed to free Leo's bonds and helped him to his feet. Leo wrapped his arms around Locke in a tight embrace.

"Whoa there . . . It's ok," Locke said. "I heard what happened. It must have been tough for you." The only thing Locke could do was to return Leo's embrace, as he tried his best to comfort his friend.

"I can explain everything later, but right now we really need to get going. It's not safe here. There are skirmishes going on all around the facility. This will be our only opportunity to escape, during all the confusion."

Releasing his embrace, Leo looked Locke in the eyes and nodded. But before Locke could manage to turn towards the door Leo stopped him. "I need to find Lily—"

Locke grabbed him by the arm and forcefully pulled him out the door. "I said I'll explain later! You'll see her again, don't worry. I still have to give that girl a piece of my mind."

Just as Leo was about to resist and demand an explanation, the sight before him left him utterly speechless. The sight before Leo, directly outside the room, was what could only be described as a massacre. The smell of blood and gore filled the hallway, making Leo instantly sick to his stomach. He averted his eyes, but as Locke quickly pulled him through the remnants of the battle, he stumbled over something.

He looked down at pieces of what once was a human torso. Seeing the fresh remains, the meager contents of Leo's stomach quickly joined the gore left by the battle.

Locke patted Leo on the back. "Don't worry, I did the same

thing when I was making my way to you. War is a terrible thing. How anyone can find enjoyment in this bloodshed is beyond me."

Leo nodded as he wiped his face and unsteadily returned to his feet. "I have a feeling we will be seeing a lot more of this kind of thing in the future. I need to get stronger. I can't get like this every time, or el—"

Locke abruptly smacked Leo on the back of the head. "It's not about being strong . . . No one should get used to this. I would rather you get sick every time you see a dead person then feel nothing at all.

"It does not make you weak. In my opinion it makes you strong. It's too easy for people to get used to it, to ignore what is happening before them. A human life is complex and mysterious; it deserves more than just to be killed. And for what? A difference of ideology? For money or power? Even people like us, created in a lab, have so much more to live for than that. If I ever see you ignore the importance of human life . . . I promise you, I'll give you way worse than a simple slap on your head."

Locke had put some serious thought into what he had just said. Leo could imagine what Locke must have seen in order to come to that opinion.

"We can't waste any more time here," Locke said. "I know a place that should be safe . . . It also just so happens that I sent Luke there ahead of us. By the time we get there everything should be ready for us to escape. Then I'll explain to you what happened." Locke retrieved two rifles from the floor and held one out to Leo. "But first I need you to take this."

Although they weren't supposed to receive their full military training until after they graduated from the academy, both Leo and Locke were familiar with the use of firearms. Though this time it was not simple training on a practice range. This time, it was for real.

When Leo placed his hands on the rifle, it was still radiating heat from recently being fired.

"It's just in case we run into any firefights on the way," Locke said. "Hopefully, we can just sneak around them. I really do not want to get into a fight with trained soldiers today. I have so many things I wanna do outside this place, after all. I decided that the first thing I want to do after all of this is see the ocean."

Leo smiled. "Oh? The first thing you wanna do is see the ocean? You know it's basically like a huge swimming pool, right? Plus, you still can't swim, you know . . ."

Leo couldn't help let out a meek smile at Locke's strange goal for after their escape.

"You think I don't know that!? I just think it would be really pretty, and seeing that may just give me the motivation to finally learn to swim." Leo laughed at his stubborn reply. "Plus," Locke whispered under his breath, "I hear that fish taste really good, so I know that a certain someone would definitely like it there. Now let's go."

They made their way cautiously through hallway after hallway. Luckily, they seemed to be always behind the battle, and neither had to fire their weapons. They plodded on in silence.

• • •

My hands are already stained with blood. Locke could not stop replaying the event in his mind. One of the reasons why he had lectured Leo earlier was because he was internally frustrated with himself.

It had happened when he was on his way to free Leo. He had been caught up in the raging battle outside the room where Leo was trapped. He had tried his best to sneak around the fighting but was still spotted by an enemy soldier.

Locke could never forget what happened next as long as he lived. He watched as the enemy leveled his gun at him. Out of sheer survival instinct Locke had raised his own weapon, but just as he was about to fire, the enemy soldier's weapon jammed. Just as Locke was about to pull the trigger, almost as if in slow motion, he saw a clear picture of the enemy soldier's face. He had an expression of utter terror, as if he had seen a runaway train screaming down the tracks towards him, and he was unable to move out of the way.

Locke hesitated, and in that moment the enemy soldier drew his side arm, and two distinctive shots rang out.

Locke felt the wind from the bullets as they each passed mere inches from his head. However, the sound of the two gunshots came from opposite directions. Adding to Locke's confusion, the enemy soldier fell to the floor, but Locke heard a solid thud behind him.

Locke turned. The bullet that had been fired by the enemy, instead of striking Locke, had hit a Tessera soldier who was trying to do his duty to protect who he probably thought was a lost student.

Realizing this, Locke turned and rushed over to the Tessera soldier's side. The bullet had pierced his helmet and killed him instantly. Locke could only blink in disbelief as he read the name on his savior's uniform.

Locke closed the man's eyes and he stood up, the battle still raging like a symphony of death around him. In a voice full of regret, and trying his best to hold back tears, he said, "Thank you, Sergeant Briggs, I promise you . . . I won't ever hesitate again." The noise from the battle was so deafening that no one around him, not even he, could hear his solemn vow.

Locke had thought of the sergeant as a kind and honorable man and knew that Leo admired him. He knew that Leo would be proud that Sergeant Briggs had given his life honorably protecting Locke, but he still couldn't bring himself to tell Leo.

Even though he knew Leo wouldn't see Briggs's death as Locke's fault, Locke himself felt the weight of his own shame and guilt weighing down upon him. He chose to remain silent as they approached their destination.

• • •

Locke led Leo to a room on the far side of the facility that was normally used only as temporary housing for visitors to Tessera. Recently it had been converted into a barracks for the soldiers that were on their way from the west. At the moment it looked to be a makeshift shelter. As they cautiously entered, Leo couldn't see anyone inside. It wasn't until Locke called out into the seemingly empty room that children began to appear from every side.

Leo recognized most of them; they were all younger children who attended the academy. Two of the children, upon seeing Leo, rushed towards him. It appeared to Leo the pair were terrified and had been recently crying.

Leo could only grin and bear it as they launched themselves into his midsection. Why was he always the one that got shown such rough affection? Locke laughed as he began to comfort the other children.

All Leo could do was hold the small children, who were scared senseless from the sounds of the raging battle all around them. "It's going to be all right, Tyler . . . Taylor. We're safe here. The battle is on the other side of the facility. There is no reason for them to come this way; there is nothing of strategic value over here."

"Th-th-thank you, Leo . . . You actually cam-"

Just as the twins were showing their appreciation, the doors on the opposite side of the room burst open. Leo and Locke reacted instantly and pointed their weapons towards the door, however, no one entered.

"Leo! Locke! I'm over here! Please help me!" Instead of its obnoxiously happy tone, Luke's voice trembled with fear as he called out to the two by name.

The two couldn't help but to look at each other with looks of surprise on their faces. Luke was supposed to have met the two in this room with the others, but it seemed something serious must have happened.

Locke cocked his head towards the open door. Leo understood his intent and nodded back in the affirmative. He slowly pushed away the now silent twins, signaling for the rest of the children to remain where they were. He and Locke slowly made their way towards the door, weapons raised.

As Leo and Locke approached the open door, they heard the presence of multiple people in the next room. They stood ready on either side of the doorway. As they were preparing to enter, another familiar yet cold voice called out to them.

"I know you two are out there," Colonel Veers said. "Can you guess what I'm doing over here? Well, I'm currently hold-ing a rather large gun to the rather small head of a crybaby traitor. I believe you know him well. If you don't want his brain to repaint these rather ugly walls, I suggest you two throw down the weapons I'm assuming you stole and come out with your hands up."

Leo had no idea why the colonel, of all people, would be here. Even worse, he had somehow captured Luke in all the commotion. There was a battle raging around the facility, after all, and he was the commander of Tessera's military. Shouldn't he have been organizing the defense of the facility instead of focusing on some measly children?

As the two stood in silence, another cry came from the terrified Luke, begging them to come out. Locke's expression stiffened as he came to a rather cold conclusion.

"Leo, we can't save him. The colonel is just trying to get us out in the open; we can't do what he says . . ."

Leo frowned. He knew that Locke was right, but he just couldn't accept Luke's death so easily. "Weren't you the one who just hit me and told me that all life was precious? That If I ever treated a human life like it was worthless you would beat the crap out of me? Now you're telling me to just let one of my friends be killed . . . just to save ourselves. I can't do that Locke; I would regret it for the rest of my life, and I know you would too."

Locke could only mentally kick himself.

"I guess . . . No . . . You're right, Leo. I would regret it for the rest of my life if Luke died in a place like this, especially after he came to us for help."

"Aww, how touching that the three traitors care so much about each other. Where was all that loyalty when you decided to betray those who raised and took care of you? Well don't worry.

This battle is making me feel rather generous. So, I'll be sure to let you share a cell after your minds have all been erased."

The colonel's mocking only strengthened the two's resolve. They threw down their weapons and entered through the open doorway. The colonel held Luke in front of him, with his pistol pointed at Luke's right temple. To Leo's surprise, the colonel appeared to be alone. Leo had assumed that there would have been soldiers to back him up.

"You can come out now, they are unarmed," the colonel said. A large smile crossed his lips.

"All my men are currently repelling those insolent forces sent by Penrose Industries. So, in the meantime I had to call in a little special backup to deal with the likes of you two. Although, I do feel it is so much more poetic to end this way."

Leo was confused by the colonel's statement until the door behind him opened, and a familiar figure walked in, still clad in her black uniform.

Upon seeing the person he yearned to see the most, Leo blurted out her name. "Lily . . ."

Lily casually walked up to the colonel's side. With his free hand the colonel reached into his pocket and retrieved what appeared to be the same electrical device that Lily had used to knock them out earlier.

Leo couldn't help but feel nervous seeing the device that caused him the most terrible pain he had ever experienced. The twisted smile never left the colonel's face as he handed the device to Lily.

"Would you be a dear and go incapacitate them for me?" the colonel said. "Oh, and don't worry, I won't let them attack you.

I'm sure if I gave them the opportunity, they would love to tear you apart for betraying them."

The colonel glared at Leo and pressed the gun harder against the terrified Luke's head. "I can see it in your eyes, boy. Don't do anything that you would regret."

Without a word, Lily took the device from the colonel's hand and took a single step forward so that she was next to the colonel. She suddenly and without warning lunged at the colonel. She had turned so quickly that the colonel's eyes suddenly went wide with surprise.

It all happened so fast that Leo could barely comprehend what had just transpired. Lily had lunged, and a split second later the colonel's eyes rolled up into his head, and he collapsed face first onto the floor.

Locke recoiled at the sound of the colonel's skull hitting the hard floor. But only a moment later a large smile of relief formed on his once tense face. While Leo continued to look on in utter surprise, it was Lily who made the next move.

With the speed of a wild animal, Lily charged at the two as she threw the device aside. Leo flinched as she hurled herself at him. It wasn't until he saw her expression that he lowered his guard and accepted what was about to happen.

It seems I am cursed after all, was all that Leo could think to himself before he was tackled to the ground.

Finally making contact with Leo, Lily was finally able to let herself go for the first time since this whole ordeal had begun. With tears streaming down her face, Lily struggled to form words. "I-I-I-I'm so sorry Leo . . . P-P-Please don't be angry with me."

Lily's cries were muffled as she buried her face in Leo's chest. He was more confused than he had ever been in his life, but he just silently wrapped his arms around the sobbing girl. First and foremost, comforting her took precedence over everything else; his questions could wait.

Out of the corner of his eye, Leo spotted Luke, who had run up to Locke and then threw himself on the ground, as he begged for forgiveness.

It seemed that Luke was lured into this room by the colonel, and then captured under threat of harm to the children next door. Even though he had messed up Locke's carefully laid plan, Locke desperately tried to convince the sobbing Luke that the whole incident wasn't entirely his fault.

After a few minutes, both Luke and Lily regained enough composure to finally answer the questions that had been filling Leo's mind.

"It all started when I rushed off to my secret room to examine what I believed to be my secret listening devices," Lily said.

"Just like before, I overheard the colonel talking to an unknown person through the wall. They were discussing the contents of a certain secretly recorded conversation that may or may not have implicated certain individuals in acts of spying and sabotage, as well as a plan for the immediate capture and public execution of the spies.

"I had to act quickly. I devised a plan that would be the hardest thing I've ever done. I knew that there was a possibility that the people I cared most about in the world might never forgive me for what I had to do, but it was a weight I needed to bear alone.

"I met with the colonel while you two were still packing for our escape. If you were there to witness my performance, you would have given me a standing ovation." Lily gave a weak smile.

"Using my knowledge that we had been bugged, I seemingly

came clean to the colonel. Explaining what we had done and who was involved, I even gave my own personal reasons for betraying you. Not realizing that I had discovered the bugs, the colonel thought I was betraying my friends in order to gain more power and status.

"He'd probably done the same thing many times to obtain his own position, and he wholeheartedly accepted what I told him as fact. I knew, though, that in order to gain his trust completely it would take more than just words.

"To fully convince the colonel, I had to hurt you in order to, hopefully, save you from an even worse fate. Knowing that his plan was to capture and quickly execute you, I mentioned in passing how much I hated you two—so much that a fate worse than death would be appropriate for you. It played perfectly to his sadistic nature.

"Your capture gave me time to plan a possible escape for us all. I went back to our secret base and found Sarah there. She told me that an attack was imminent and to prepare myself. When the initial attack began, I used the confusion to free Locke with my mechanical creations that the colonel is so fond of.

"With Locke freed, we made a plan to secure you and meet with Luke at this location to escape during the ensuing battle. Things did not go quite as we planned."

Locke turned to Leo and said, "The battle slowed my progress making my way to free you. Then, somehow the colonel was tipped off to part of our escape plan, and Luke was captured. The only reason things didn't fall apart completely was the fact that the colonel kept Lily by his side after the battle began, in order to keep an eye on his newly acquired asset."

Leo remained dead silent as he intently listened to what had happened. He patiently waited as the story finally reached the present. "Lily, tell me how—

A single gunshot pierced the air.

With their ears ringing, they all turned to face the awakened and still-armed Colonel Veers. He was about fifteen feet away. His face was covered in blood from where he had hit the ground, and his eyes were ablaze with rage. With all the commotion going on, all four of them had forgotten to restrain the colonel.

"I should have expected this . . . I got careless. . . But lucky for me you all were just as careless and didn't finish me off." He raised his gun again and pointed it directly at Leo.

Thankfully, the colonel was still shaky on his feet from being knocked out and had missed his first shot. He was not the kind of man to take warning shots.

Leo, Locke, and Lily simultaneously sprinted in different directions. Even for an experienced soldier like the colonel, it would be hard to hit three moving targets traveling in different directions, especially in his current condition.

Locke pulled out a utility knife he had concealed within his pocket and threw it squarely at the colonel's head. Veers fired a single shot before raising his weapon to block the knife. In a testament to the colonel's training and skill, his shot had not missed.

Although the shot was on target, it was Luke who began to stagger, as blood pooled on the ground where he stood, arms spread, in front of Leo.

What happened next could only be described as a blur. Locke closed the distance and managed to grab the gun, forcefully jamming it. Now unable to fire his weapon again, the colonel reacted by swinging with his free hand, knocking Locke to the floor. The gun bounced out of his grasp and slid under a nearby storage crate.

While this was happening, Leo caught the falling Luke. Lily rushed over to their side. From the amount of blood gushing from the wound in Luke's chest the shot appeared to be a fatal one. Leo and Lily tried desperately to stop the bleeding. They had both treated injuries before but nothing like this. No matter what they did, nothing seemed to help. Luke looked up at them with eye's like glass. The more ragged his breathing became, the more desperate Leo grew. As he was applying pressure to the wound, he reassured Luke.

"It's going to be all right, Luke. It's just a scratch. You're going to be just fine. You're going to be just fine. You'll be just—"

A cold hand grasped his trembling arm. Luke moved his head to face Leo. His glazed-over eyes momentarily regained their former sparkle, as he spoke in a soft and eerily calm voice.

"This was the first thing I have ever done that I wasn't told to do beforehand. It felt good to be able to make that choice for once. I know you don't want to hear it, but you are special . . . More than I could ever be . . . You three need to live. I don't know if you're meant to change the world or not, but can I ask you guys one thing?"

Tears flowed down the faces of both Leo and Lily as they nodded their heads, hands stilled pressed on Luke's wound.

"Please stay the same as you are now. Don't let this cruel world change you. Please try to remember me as a good fr—"

Luke's voice suddenly stopped as his head slumped lifelessly to one side. Leo released his hands from the wound and instead grabbed Luke's head. "Luke! Stay with us! What were you going to say? Stay with us!"

Leo shook Luke's limp head as if trying to wake him from a deep sleep. Realizing Luke would never wake up again, Leo looked into his friend's eye's one last time and began to scream. It was an inhuman scream, as if an injured animal were calling out for his pack mates.

He looked around himself with new eyes. His mind, so full of sorrow, was now filled with a pure rage. His eyes found their target. The colonel was gripping Locke by the collar and savagely beating him senseless.

Leo released Luke's head and stood up. His entire body felt like it was going to be ripped apart by the torrent of anger building within him. He felt as though if he did not act now, the sheer pressure would cause him to explode.

Resting between Leo and the colonel was the knife that had been deflected from its target. Perhaps sensing movement, the colonel turned. His gaze met Leo's eyes and then darted to the knife on the ground between them.

They both rushed for it, but with the last of his strength, Locke managed to grip the colonel's leg just enough to slow him down momentarily before he kicked free.

Leo felt the cold steel enter his hands as he and the colonel fell to the ground. A new, warmer sensation enveloped his hands. Leo looked down and saw where the knife had plunged into the colonel's chest.

Leo felt the movement of the colonel gasping for breath beneath him. A dark desire consumed Leo's entire being. He pulled out the knife and raised his arm to plunge the blade down again into his mortal enemy.

Locke grabbed his arm from behind, stopping it midswing.

His voice sounded on the verge of tears, and he gripped Leo's arm.

"Leo, you won . . . That is a fatal wound. There's no need to do any more."

Leo barely heard the words in his rage. The only thing that was registering was the overwhelming need for vengeance for everything that had been done to him. He desperately fought back against the hand that was gripping him. As he struggled, he let out another animalistic yell in frustration.

A smug smile crossed the colonel's pained face. "Even in defeat, it seems I have won just a slight consolation. Congratulations, Leo. You have finally met my expectations . . ."

Even as the colonel breathed his last, Leo still struggled against Locke's grip. It wasn't until he felt a sharp pain on the back of his head that he finally came back to his senses.

Just as he said he would, Locke had punched the back of Leo's head with what little force he had left. Leo finally realized what he had just done. He dropped the knife and began to cry. All he could do was look down at his own hands, which were covered with blood.

He now understood what the colonel had meant. There could be no turning back now. As a wave of insurmountable guilt began to crash over him, he felt two pairs of hands struggle to pull him out of the water.

Lily and Locke wrapped their arms around Leo, as he continued to cry. The three might not have been related by blood, but at this moment they shared something that was even more rare.

Locked arm in arm, the trio cried. They cried for the loss of their friend, they cried for the loss of their old lives, and they cried for the potential happiness that they all so desperately wanted.

All their emotions began to mix together—anger, sadness, happiness, and regret. No longer would they have to bear any of them alone, for they were a family.

EPILOGUE

THE DOORS TO THE ROOM burst open and soldiers entered, guns drawn. They quickly surrounded Leo and his companions, who were huddled over Luke's body. Accompanying them was the face of someone familiar, however, Sarah was now dressed in what appeared to be a Penrose uniform, sporting many ribbons and stripes. Seeing what they had done, Sarah dismissed the soldiers, who saluted and promptly left the room.

"Thank you, guys, for making my job a lot easier. Killing the colonel was supposed to be my job. Well, I think you should know that Penrose has secured almost the entire facility. With the colonel dead and Director Anderson having fled the facility, it seems that the battle is ours. So, congratulations, I will be sure to write about your actions in my report."

The three looked up at her and then looked at each other. They were battered, bloody, and covered in tears.

"It's finally over?" Leo said. "We can leave?"

"It seems that way . . . Penrose will be taking over this facility. You won't be forced to stay here of course, but it won't be like it was before, if you do choose to stay."

Locke tried his best to speak up, however his face had become so swollen that all he could manage was a single word, "ocean." Leo couldn't help but smile as he wiped the tears from his face.

"I think it's about time we go see the outside world," Leo said. "I've had enough of living in this place. There are so many things we need to see and do, after all."

Lily and Locke nodded their heads adamantly in approval.

"As long as I can work on my creations I don't care if we head to the other side of the world!" Lily said. "I hope they have good technology over by this ocean place."

For the first time since this whole ordeal started, Sarah broke out into a fit of genuine laughter. "Well it just so happens that the base where I'm from is located right on the coast. I am heading back there after we finish up here. I could bring you guys with me if you would like. I know I haven't been particularly kind to you three, but now that Tessera's beaten and I'm not worried about my mission anymore, I would like to make it up to you."

"I don't know . . ." Leo said.

Both Lily and Locke anxiously looked at him, waiting for his answer. It wasn't until he saw the two hopeful expressions on his companions' faces that Leo finally cracked.

"I guess it would be all right. But only if you lead us there, and then we can go our own way after we reach the ocean."

Sarah laughed again. "Sure, whatever you say, kid. But I have a feeling that after you see our base you might change your mind. Well, before we get underway you guys need to freshen up; you are all in really rough shape. Both Leo and Locke look like they require medical attention."

Finally managing to stifle her laughter, Sarah called for a few of her men to bring in stretchers.

"All right you two, it's obvious you can't walk on your own, so we'll take you to the medical area we have set up."

Begrudgingly, both Leo and Locke allowed themselves to be helped onto stretchers. They were carried to a guarded room that was full of those injured during the fighting. Lily followed them and insisted that the soldiers bring Luke's body with them.

• • •

While Locke was being placed down onto a medical cot, he couldn't help but look over at Leo, who had fallen asleep from sheer exhaustion on the journey over. In comparison with the animalistic expression Leo had been making a few minutes ago, his face was calm, and he was now peacefully snoring away.

Locke was happy that they had all managed to survive, but there was a small nagging thought in the back of his mind. He had never in his life witnessed Leo snap like he had when he fought the colonel.

Locke only hoped that it was a onetime thing, but he couldn't help thinking about what would have happened if he hadn't been there to stop Leo. What would happen next time?

He shook off the thought. *As long as I am there by his side, I won't have to worry about it. As long as we are all together, he'll be just fine.* But even as he tried desperately to convince himself, he saw the body of Luke, who had been brought in with them.

Locke stared at Luke's body. Even though he never really considered him a close friend, he still couldn't help feeling sad. Just like with Sergeant Briggs, it felt as if even more weight was being added to the guilt on his conscience. If he felt this way, he knew that Lily must feel the same way and, Leo, even more so.

Locke tried his best to understand his own feelings, as his exhausted body began to drift off to sleep. Just before he closed his eyes, he saw the bright face of Lily. Not too long ago she had asked him for acting lessons. She really did take his lessons seriously. *The most important rule of acting . . . No matter what happens, always keep smiling.*

• • •

Lily watched her two sleeping friends. She always tried her best to hide her negative feelings with a smile, but now her facade broke completely, and she began to cry. However, her tears were not of sadness but of joy.

The one thing that she learned from their ordeal was that she had an inherent ability to smile no matter how she felt on the inside. She realized that if she could just keep that smile, no matter what else was going on around them, both Leo and Locke would feed off her, and they would keep their own smiles.

After so long feeling like they were always protecting her, Lily now felt as though she finally knew her purpose within the group. No matter what, she would keep her smile for the sake of her friends. She cried because, even after all that she had done, she was happy. She cried because she was finally where she belonged, right here with her true family.

• • •

Leo awoke to the sounds of celebration and woke Lily and Locke in turn. They learned that all of Tessera's troops had fled the facility, and the Penrose troops were in high spirits. Finally released from the medical area, they were allowed to return to their rooms to retrieve their belongings.

On the way, they passed remnants of the huge battle that had taken place. Progress was slow, as they struggled to move through the corridors. Rubble and weapons of war blocked their path many times, and it took most of the day for them to reach their rooms and gather their meager belongings for the trip to Penrose's base.

Lily practically dragged Leo and Locke to retrieve Rusty. They would not have heard the end of it if they had chosen to leave him behind. As day turned to evening, they finally headed back, with Rusty happily trotting behind them. On their way they were met by Sarah, who insisted that they join her.

Without knowing where they were going, they obeyed and followed her while still carrying their packed bags. When they reached the central elevator, Sarah turned to them and coyly pointed her index finger up.

"I think it's about time that I showed you guys what a sunset looks like." Sarah looked at her watch. "Today was supposed to be clear, so hopefully it will be visible."

Leo definitely liked this version of Sarah better than he had before. It had been almost like she had pretended to be Ms. Meli for so long that, even when she wasn't acting, bits and pieces of that old personality still shone through. Leo laughed to himself as they got into the elevator.

When they reached the top floor, they exited out onto the former military checkpoint at surface level. The trio had never been to this floor before, and they excitedly looked around as Sarah called a military truck to their location.

The four entered, and Rusty happily jumped in the back as the huge metal double door of the facility creaked to life. Sunlight flooded inside, and they had to cover their eyes as the truck set off through the open entranceway.

Leo had no idea what to expect for their first time outside, but the moment they exited the facility's walls his mouth dropped open. After spending their entire lives within the underground facility, for the first time they could see the vast sky, slightly tinted orange by the setting sun.

The facility entrance was on the side of a rather large mountain. They traveled for a few more minutes in utter awe before the truck came to a sudden halt at the edge of a barren cliff.

Sarah snapped them out of their trance as she shoved them out of the truck and paraded them to the edge. The view was breathtaking. They stood overlooking a small, forested valley, with the setting sun picturesque in the distance.

They watched as the light slowly faded from the terrain. Leo silently wished that this moment would last forever, and he felt two hands grip his own, as the final traces of light left the sky.

As night replaced the day and darkness filled the valley below, faint lights could be made out in the distance. They seemed to be getting closer or brighter as Leo watched, wondering what they were. The lights seemed to multiply, and a light much brighter than the others approached their position at a tremendous speed. For the first time since he had been built, Rusty gave a loud bark from the bed of the truck.

The bright light seemed to gain even more speed as it raced towards them. As the light became blinding, Sarah quickly grabbed them and pulled them back into the truck. The bright light screamed past them and hit the side of the mountain in a tremendous explosion.

The truck's radio crackled to life, and frantic voices could be heard. As they huddled together in the back of the truck, they strained to understand the overlapping voices on the radio. Then the entire mountainside began to tremble violently from seemingly inside the mountain itself. At that instant, all radio chatter eerily stopped. A few tense seconds of radio static passed, broken by a single intelligible word before the radio finally gave out.

"Tessera."

BONUS CHAPTER

A SOLDIER'S SACRIFICE

I **TRIED MY HARDEST TO STIFLE A LARGE GROAN** as I performed my assigned duty. Today I was the sole guard, standing in front of the command center of Tessera's easternmost facility. It wasn't the worst job I had ever been assigned, but it was not what I would consider particularly exciting. Since the command center was located deep within the heart of the facility, there was basically zero chance that anything exciting would ever happen. We were located within one of Tessera's strongest facilities, after all. "Standing guard" was more for show than anything else.

Fighting my more slothful urges, I kept a straight face as I checked some officers' clearance cards before allowing them through the command center's thick steel doors.

"Thank you, Sergeant Briggs," said one of them, reading my name tag.

I hadn't been on my shift more than ten minutes, and I was already about to keel over. I wanted to go back to my nice, cozy bed so badly.

Even though I'd been a soldier for almost my entire life, I still hated waking up whenever I had an early guard shift. Truthfully, I would consider myself a low-energy person. If I lived in any other period in history, I doubt that I would have ever chosen soldier as a career path. If anything, I would have much preferred being a connoisseur. I had no idea what it was, but the name sure sounded relaxing.

The only reason I was even standing guard at all and not suffering a fate worse than death out in the Wasteland was due to Tessera. Though I would consider myself a slacker by nature, I had a duty to repay them for all the organization had done for me. Without them taking me in as a mere starving child in the Wasteland, I would have surely died an all-too-common death in my rathole of a village. I had been abandoned by my family and left to die; I couldn't thank Tessera enough for saving me.

Though I felt military life directly clashed with my personality, it was the job I was assigned by my saviors. I could not afford to disappoint them. I had to repay them for all the kindness they had shown me when they pulled me from the wreckage and devastation that had been my daily life.

The irony of my situation wasn't lost on me at all. Even though I greatly disliked being a soldier, I seemed to be a competent one. I had even been promoted to the rank of sergeant, which was very unusual for someone not born within Tessera itself. All my superiors always complimented my abilities. They especially liked my general demeanor, for some reason. I never really understood what they were talking about, but they always said I was "extremely imposing," and that I had "intimidating eyes," perfect for being a guard. Which to me never really made any sense, because I was always the one that felt intimidated whenever a superior officer would even acknowledge my existence. However, as time went on I just kind of got used to it. So, as of late, I was one of the facility's best guard dogs. Since I looked the part so well, I was always placed in Omega-level areas in the facility, such as the command center or the top secret forty-seventh floor.

You would be surprised by how much information you could pick up by just standing in front of a highly secure area. Listening to bits and pieces of conversations day after day from those I would let inside really opened my eyes to what Tessera's true purpose was and how far the powers that be would go to achieving its goals.

I would be the first person to admit that Tessera wasn't perfect. Like any organization with a large population, things could get a bit chaotic and cruel. But in comparison to my childhood in the Wasteland, where starvation, murder, and unspeakable acts were committed daily, Tessera was a mystical land full of boundless resources and righteousness.

Since most of its members were not from the outside world, they were always prone to be discriminatory towards those who were either conscripted or joined of their own free will. A part of me could understand why. After partaking in my share of horrific battles against the likes of the cultists and other malevolent organizations, I understood their resentment was partially justified. Still, it was probably my biggest complaint with Tessera as a whole.

Unlike areas under Tessera's control, the outside world was an utter disaster. Though I found absolutely no enjoyment in killing others, I understood why Tessera was forceful in their steady conquest of the world. It was all in the vein of bringing peace and stability back to the world by any means necessary. I saw Tessera as a truly benevolent, utilitarian organization.

I quickly stifled a small yawn as a group of three small figures in academy uniforms came walking down the hallway towards me. It was pretty strange that students from the academy would be in this area of the facility. I couldn't help thinking they were lost. They looked pretty young.

However, before I could ponder the matter any further, they approached me, and I stiffened my posture as I went through my usual guard routine. Now that I was examining the trio closer, I could see that they appeared to be students, but they were anything but normal children. These three were something special; I had never seen anything like them.

While the boy that seemed to be the leader of the small group told me his reasoning for approaching me, I finally understood why I sensed this strange aura around them. That was the first time I noticed the insignia on their academy uniforms, numbers one through three.

I couldn't believe it. Instantly, I remembered what I had overheard while I had been guarding the top secret forty-seventh floor some time ago. At that time, most of the information I overheard from those coming and going had been about three amazing children, often referred to as "experiments." How they were the first round of clones to ever reach full autonomy and pass all physical, psychological, and genetic compatibility testing. How they were supposed to be Tessera's future. I never really understood what they meant.

However, even someone of just average intelligence like me could tell that, the way they were being talked about, these three were viewed more as test subjects than living, breathing children. Some of the more gruesome details about their history were quite shocking. However, at the time, I had no real concept of what I was overhearing, so I just always assumed that I was misunderstanding the small bits and pieces out of context.

But witnessing the three in person, a lot of the random information I had heard made more sense. The mere fact that this young boy had been summoned by Colonel Veers, of all people, meant that he was indeed very special. Even I had only ever directly spoken to the man once before, and I stood guard in front of the command center that housed his office.

Though he had a meeting with the colonel, I could sense from the trio's demeanor and tone that they were extremely nervous and rightfully so. I had no idea why they had been summoned, but a meeting with the colonel was never usually a pleasant affair. The sole time I had ever spoken to him, I was forced to face him for punishment after I had broken military protocol. That was when I learned how truly terrifying Director Anderson's right-hand man could be.

Though it was my duty to let the young boy named Leo inside to meet his fate, I couldn't help silently wishing him luck as he vanished inside the command center.

It was now the end of my shift, and I had just been relieved from my post. I wasn't overly nervous or anything, but I couldn't shake an odd feeling. I had been standing guard for some time after letting Leo in, yet the boy had not left the command center.

What had further piqued my curiosity was the fact that I had witnessed the colonel leave the command center with a group of officers only a few minutes after I had let the young boy in to see him. It was rather strange that, after all this time, he had never emerged, even after the man he was supposed to see had left.

That was when I did something that I would not have usually done. I was not normally one to get attached to people or things, but for some reason I sympathized with those three children. I had heard so much about them thirdhand that putting faces to the rumors had made me more than a little interested in them.

Under the guise of delivering something to the colonel's office, I made my way inside the command center. It was rather hard to search for the kid while trying to keep a low profile, but in the end, I managed to find the boy.

Sadly, my hunch was correct. A meeting with the colonel only ever meant one thing—a painful lesson needed to be learned.

I couldn't help feeling for the boy after seeing his pathetic state. He had experienced being "retrained." In layman's terms, he had suffered one hell of a beating. It had been so bad that he appeared to have lost consciousness.

Thankfully, when I entered the room it seemed like he was starting to come to. I couldn't help smiling to myself as I checked on the boy. He was a resilient one, that much was obvious. Even after the beating he had received, he appeared to bounce right back. That, or he was trying his utmost to put on a tough-guy act. Either way, I was amused by this unique child.

For some reason, this boy named Leo had a familiar aura about him. I could not quite place it. But when he looked at me, his eyes full of surprise at my presence, I could not shake the feeling I had seen those exact same eyes somewhere before. It felt like they belonged to someone important to me.

Sadly, I didn't remember much from my childhood in the Wasteland. Was it a sibling? My parents? A friend? But no matter how hard I tried to remember, it eluded me. Helping Leo to his feet, I tried to push those thoughts out of my mind.

I thought I hadn't been spotted as I wandered around looking for Leo. I was woefully mistaken. Just as the two of us had finished saying our good-byes, and I had parted ways with the interesting boy, I was unceremoniously ambushed by a rather stern-faced officer. Sadly, he was an officer I knew well. His name was Miller, and for some reason unknown to me, he held quite a poor opinion of me.

I had little choice in the matter as he dragged me all the way to the colonel's location. I knew I was in for it. I had not only snuck into the colonel's office, but I had also helped someone who the colonel had punished directly, both of which were serious offenses.

Even though it was wildly out of character for me to break the rules, despite hearing the colonel's rage-filled voice and feeling his swift blow, I did not feel guilty. I knew deep down that what I had done was the right thing. Despite the fact I got into a world of trouble for it, I would have gladly done it again, just to see the expression on that young boy's face.

Mimicking the situation Leo had just been in, now it was me who was face down on the dirty floor. Unlike for Leo, however, no one came for me. That didn't really bother me; I had been expecting as much.

As I was lying there, my pain-filled mind had remembered something. I couldn't believe I had forgotten. I couldn't believe that I had forgotten about him, even after all this time. How could I have forgotten about my own little brother?

At that moment my physical pain was nothing compared to the new wave of emotional pain that crashed over me. However, it wasn't just a single wave of emotion. Now that the floodgates were open, my old memories wouldn't stop flooding back.

It felt as though I was about to burst at the seams. It hadn't just been my little brother I had forgotten about. Friends, family, my most cherished memories, all forgotten. No, stolen.

There was no way I would have forgotten all of this. Tessera, they must have stolen my memories. They must have done something to me.

My head was spinning. The last seventeen years of my life were nothing more than an elaborate lie. I had no idea what to believe anymore. A part of me wished that I had suffered a concussion and was hallucinating all of this, but another part of me knew it was 100 percent true.

Finally gaining the strength to get on my feet, I was no longer the hawk-eyed but lazy soldier I once was. Now, I was a completely new person. I had my old memories, my current abilities, and a new goal.

But before I could fulfill my new goal, I had to take care of some minor details first, one of which would lead me to stumble upon a certain red-haired teacher, a spy who just so happened to have a very similar goal to mine.

Funny enough, we almost killed each other at first, but after exchanging a few verbal jabs using knives, we came to a mutually beneficial deal. Since I was a guard and could gain access, I would steal her a map of the facility from the archives. Then with the help of the map, she would coordinate with her allies on the outside to help me accomplish my new goal of freeing myself of the ones who erased my memories and forced me into becoming their willing slave.

. . .

It came as a welcome surprise when I heard the news of the incident at the Founding Celebration. I wish I could have been there to witness the chaos firsthand. But now that my plan was set in motion, I wouldn't have to wait very long.

Still, fulfilling my normal duties as a soldier was growing insufferable. I hated pretending to be complacent, as I completed my meaningless assignments. However, during my next guard rotation outside the command center, I was again caught completely by surprise.

The catalyst for the return of my long-lost memories had suddenly appeared before me, with his two companions in tow. Truthfully, I never imagined that I would see them again so soon.

It was strange. They were only children, but I still felt slightly self-conscious as they approached. Lowering my helmet slightly so they wouldn't recognize me, I attempted to avoid their notice.

I underestimated them. They recognized me almost instantly. Though I had trouble looking the young boy named Leo in the eyes, I managed to get through our brief conversation.

It was strange. Here I was, an adult looking down at a young child, beyond nervous because he had unknowingly helped me to regain my long-lost past. I didn't know if I felt indebted to him or just embarrassed by the fact that someone half my own age had caused all of this to happen. Maybe after getting my memories back, my personality was changing.

Thankfully, our meeting was short lived. I didn't know if I could have held back my awkwardness around them if it had been any longer.

The universe definitely has a sense of humor. The very next day, just as I thought I had seen the last of those three strange children, I was called into the command center. I assumed it was for more punishment, but surprisingly, I was wrong. It was much worse than I could have ever imagined.

I was ordered by the director himself to go and fetch those same three children, Leo, Lily, and Locke. I couldn't believe it. Of all people, I had to be the one ordered to retrieve them and bring them to the director. My only hope was that they turned out not to be home.

I almost preemptively breathed a sigh of relief when the first two appeared not to be home, but when I reached the residence of Leo, my chest tightened when the door opened. I hated it, the way they acted. It resembled how I used to act with my own siblings. What made it all the worse was the one called Leo even slightly resembled one of my long-lost younger brothers.

The whole time I escorted them I couldn't help feeling slightly jealous. I had no idea if my own family was still alive, but as I continued to watch the trio's interactions, I felt a deep peace wash over me.

Their mood was infectious, especially the sole girl of the group, Lily. I instantly took a liking to her. She was obviously strong-willed and quick-witted when it came to dealing with the other two. It must have been due to the fact she was the only girl among their little group. The longer we walked, the more I began to relax. Before I realized it, Lily and I had gone off on multiple, detailed tangents about this and that in our conversation.

For the first time in a long time, I thoroughly enjoyed myself. When our journey reached its conclusion, I was quite sad. For a brief moment it felt as though I had experienced what it was like to return to my life before Tessera, before all that I cherished was hidden from me.

The circumstances didn't matter to me. I would be forever

indebted to these three children. This time, when I finally waved goodbye, I wished it would not be the last time I would see them. Sadly, I knew the fate that would soon befall the facility, and I wished for them to survive it. Steeling my resolve, I came to an internal decision. When the battle with Penrose began, I would try my hardest to make sure that Leo, Lily, and Locke survived.

Though I would never get the chance to know the fruits of my sacrifice, I had indeed fulfilled my goal. My sacrifice was not in vain. Even if I had known what would befall me, I would have gladly done it all over again. I guess I was a pretty good soldier after all . . .

AFTERWORD

Hey! It's me, Stephen, here! I can't thank you enough for picking up my first-ever published work! Wow . . . I can't even believe I just typed those words out. It's been a long time coming!

I hope you enjoyed reading this book just as much as I enjoyed writing it. Strangely enough, it didn't feel so much like I was creating a story but rather that I was recording one. It's weird to say, but to me all the characters in this story feel almost real. It felt just like I was remembering something that had already happened. In that vein, I have already started recording the sequel and even beyond. How will Leo, Lily, and Locke survive in the outside world? Will they finally be able to escape Tessera's clutches? Well, if you want to find all that out, you should consider picking up the next volumes in the series when they come out. At this time writing is just a hobby of mine, indulged around my full-time engineering job. But knowing me, my fingers won't stop typing until this wild ride comes to an amazing end.

Funnily enough, every time I keep trying to figure out how long this series is going to be, it just keeps getting bigger and bigger. First it was going to be a trilogy, now . . . I'm not so sure.

Maybe five? Maybe more? If there's one thing I'm not short of, it's plenty of ideas.

I want to thank all the people in my life that helped make this possible: my family and friends, who helped by reading my earliest drafts; my amazing artist; and my editor. Without all of you and your support, this book would never have somehow materialized from a dude who can barely spell a simple word without having to check Google.

Until the next time!

Stephen B. Gresko

Made in the USA
Las Vegas, NV
24 November 2023

81420464R00132